The D

The Deceitful Marriage

and

The Dialogue of the Dogs

Miguel de Cervantes

Translated by William Rowlandson

ET REMOTISSIMA PROPE

Hesperus Classics

Hesperus Classics
Published by Hesperus Press Limited
4 Rickett Street, London SW6 1RU
www.hesperuspress.com

'The Deceitful Marriage' first published in Spanish as '*El casamiento engañoso*' in 1613;
'The Dialogue of the Dogs' first published in Spanish as '*El coloquio de los perros*' in 1613
This translation first published by Hesperus Press Limited, 2004

Introduction and English language translation © William Rowlandson, 2004
Foreword © Ben Okri, 2004

Designed and typeset by Fraser Muggeridge
Printed in Italy by Graphic Studio Srl

ISBN: 1-84391-065-9

CONTENTS

You can tell the greatness of an artist by the greatness of the challenge which they set themselves, and which they conceal from us, and which they rise to with apparent ease. There is nothing more enlightening than to watch the hands of a master at work on a small canvas. The mind of an artist is never so clear as when they are working in miniature, nor more obscure. In *The Dialogue of the Dogs* it is fascinating to see how Cervantes enters into a subject, how he sublimates himself in it, how he occupies it, in a ghostly fashion. It is marvellous to behold how he employs the art of mirror thinking, of fiction through internal dialogues, and his plain love for the impossible. He loves to mirror the world through odd angles and tangents, to see the world through innocent-seeming eyes impregnated with a satirical vision. He is the true creator: he is at home in all that can be a receptacle of consciousness and reflective vision.

This is essentially a refractive tale. It is a classic world within a world, worlds interpenetrating worlds, each one qualifying and questioning the other. The fictional relativity at work in this double- helix narrative could only have come from the fiendish and miraculous spirit of the man who created *Don Quixote*, one of the most fascinating and beautiful novels of all time. *The Dialogue of the Dogs* should be seen not as an introduction to *Don Quixote* or to the author's mind, but as a work worthy of profound study and meditation in its own right. All Cervantes' great themes are here. The ineluctability of reality; the mystery of speech; the impossibility of true communication; the relativity of truth; the irony of consciousness; the vast gap between appearance and reality; and the illusory nature of the world as we think it or perceive it to be.

Only Cervantes would dream of appending such a wonderfully rich fiction of two dogs talking to a perfectly satisfying tale of trickery and deception. Beginning with the familiar, the cunning master lures us into an even deeper familiarity, and then plays a great trick on our minds – he makes us forget that we are doing the unthinkable; that we are actually overhearing two dogs talking about us; about our doings; about the follies and treacheries of the human condition. He makes us accept a condition of madness. We find ourselves eavesdropping on talking dogs. This, under normal circumstances, would make us certifiable. As you read this tale, you come to the peculiar conclusion that human beings are all a little mad; that there is something not quite right about us on account of what we do not question, or think about, or look into deeply enough. The dogs show us that maybe the fact that we possess the gift of speech does not mean we are as intelligent as we think. This is both a disquieting and a salubrious reading experience. Only an artist who suffered the folly and stupidities, the cupidities and mean-mindedness of humanity, and who still has a great heart and a profound sense of humour could have conceived and executed such an intriguing gaze into the human condition. For within these linked tales there is a great spirit of laughter.

Do not be discouraged by the substantial bulk of its apparent form. Like all true works of art it can be enjoyed in bite sizes, as well as in great swallows. *The Dialogue of the Dogs* is an essential work not only of literature but of the human spirit. It is to be enjoyed, to be laughed with, and used to inspire sober meditations on our condition as we would never think to see ourselves, from the viewpoint of those who see us most clearly at our best and our worst. You may never look at a dog the same way again. In fact, you may never look at any animal the same way again. We are being watched by innumerable mute eyes. We are more transparent than we think.

This novella also brings together so many sides of Cervantes' genius. In it you can also see the playwright at work. This is visible in his masterful and ingenious use of the art of dialogue. There is such a rich orchestration of pleasures in the dialogues between the dogs. Part of the joy of reading the story is in the brilliance of the dialogues themselves. It must be remembered that Cervantes was also an accomplished playwright who wrote more than twenty plays. This little-known aspect of his range accounts for one of the many unsung felicities of *Don Quixote*, which is the sheer delicious nature of the dialogues between Sancho Panza and the eponymous hero. Indeed, dialogue is a crucial instrument in the massive orchestra of that great novel. In this tale, it is an instrument as ambiguous and flexible as a bassoon or a French horn. And it is deployed with great concentrated effect. Its purpose is to make us *listen* more intensely.

It is worth pointing out that one of the dogs (Berganza) has a racial bias and tells the story of a love-hungry Negress that makes one squirm. The dogs are also awkward about Jews and Moors, but at least their prejudice reveals the presence of different races in the Spain of the times. Western literature, on the whole, perplexes the spirit with many unfortunate attitudes to black people, Jews and Moors. It is hard to bypass this fact without comment; it fairly ruins much reading that might have been a pleasure and if one were to succumb to annoyance there is much one would never read. Fortunately here it is not too serious, passes quickly, and one can proceed into the depths of the tale after a little sweat of embarrassment. This is much worse in *Don Quixote*, and only the greatness of the text makes us overlook such grievances.

The Dialogue of the Dogs is a cunning tale within a tale, full of fictional puns and mental mischief, framed by that great device through which improbable things are made plausible by the dimensions within the narrative – a favourite as much of playwrights as of painters, as can be seen in the mysterious works of Velázquez. And so the colloquy which comes to occupy the mind is a device, and talking dogs are presented as beyond dispute. This is the power of the magic frame.

Someone ought to make a film out of this tale, for it lives so splendidly in the mind's eye, as much when reading it as in remembrance.

– *Ben Okri, 2004*

Having during his life been a soldier, a captive, a revenue collector for the Invincible Armada and a prisoner; following the publication in 1605 of the first part of *Don Quixote*, Cervantes became a writer by profession: no longer merely desiring to be popular, he *needed* to be popular. From the pastoral romance of *La Galatea*, to the two parts of *Don Quixote*, to *Las Novelas ejemplares* [*The Exemplary Novels*], Cervantes' work is characterised by an engaging, earthy and vital narrative, of a style that would have been at once familiar to his readers, whether as reminiscent of the chivalric epic, the pastoral, or the widely popular picaresque novel. To this day, what most astonishes those reading Cervantes for the first time is his immense readability, his rich and often bawdy humour, the compelling characterisation, tangible realism and visionary fantasy. Cervantes is, first and foremost, a master storyteller.

And yet, 'All art is at once surface and symbol,' declared Oscar Wilde. 'Those who go beneath the surface do so at their peril.' Cervantes' immense popularity cannot be solely attributable to an entertaining style and a gripping tale: the scope of possible meaning and interpretation of his writing is vast. This is abundantly true in 'The Dialogue of the Dogs', a tale of the wandering adventures of an unusually wise dog, which, beyond an engaging adventure, embodies many of the literary and philosophical questions encountered in Cervantes' most celebrated work, *Don Quixote*.

'The Dialogue of the Dogs' is included in the collection of tales entitled *Las Novelas ejemplares*. In the very title of this collection, the ironical humour of Cervantes is at once discernible. The *novela* was a genre of Italian heritage and was predominantly a short, ribald and anecdotal story. *Libros de ejemplos*, however, were of a more serious moral, ethical and didactic content, dating back to Aesop and familiar in Spain through, for example, the work of Don Juan Manuel, author of *El Conde Lucanor*. The two genres had never been fused before, giving the title of Cervantes' tales an oxymoronic intrigue. This factor would have encouraged the reader firstly to consider these *novelas* in greater depth than the genre had hitherto demanded, and secondly to expect some edifying lesson within the tales.

These stories, however, do not conclude with the same didactic proverbs of earlier *ejemplar* tales. In the prologue, Cervantes explains to his 'most amiable reader' that all readers should be able 'to draw out some useful and profitable example', and that, had he more time, he would reveal 'the tasty and honest fruit that one may draw out, as much from the tales as a whole, as from each tale individually'. In certain tales, like 'The Force of Blood', the conclusion to the plot runs so contrary to expectation that the instructive *ejemplo* is far from clear. In others, like 'The Jealous Extremaduran', the *ejemplo* offered by the narrative may be deemed too simplistic, demanding a more rigorous reading of the text. Thus the reader is encouraged to employ full intellectual and interpretative skill to 'draw out' the work's instructive discourse.

'The Deceitful Marriage' and 'The Dialogue of the Dogs' are the final stories of the collection and the two combine to form one, with the narrative of the first introducing and concluding the second. In the first, the Licentiate Peralta runs into his long-lost friend, the Ensign Campuzano, and, seeing the latter's pitiful condition, invites him home to share a meal and to recount his misfortunes. Campuzano's tale concerns a marriage based on false appearances, greed and deceit which ends with a synoptic Italian proverb in verse. Campuzano, however, explains that his misfortune was indeed good fortune, as it led him to overhearing the dialogue that forms the second, lengthier tale. Thus the first brief narrative serves the important function of engaging the listener, awakening his credulity and enticing him into the proceeding tale.

The dialogue that the convalescent ensign overheard at night was between two dogs, unexpectedly granted the gift of speech and human reason. To profit by this, they decide to tell each other their life stories, beginning that night with Berganza's, and continuing the following night (should they still have the gift) with Scipio's. Campuzano writes this in the form of a colloquy, or written dialogue, and sleeps while the licentiate reads it.

The tale displays from the outset certain characteristics of the picaresque novels popular at the time. Firstly, like other works, this is the rendition (and confession) of the protagonist's life up to the present point. The protagonist is usually of unknown parentage, travels widely, serves many masters, is capable of terrible (although justified) cruelty, is regularly starved and beaten and occasionally lavishly rewarded, only to be plunged once again into misfortune. More importantly, the picaresque hero observes and provides a philo-sophising commentary on the events experienced and witnessed. Yet to define the colloquy merely as a classic example of this style, or as a straight satire of it, would likewise be to limit *Don Quixote* to a mere satire of the chivalric works read by the former hidalgo. It would similarly be a limitation to read the colloquy as a litany of complaints against the elements of society that Berganza encounters along his travels. For although the scorn heaped upon the slaughterhouse men, the shepherds, the bailiff and notary, the witch, gypsies, Moriscos and poets is venomous and ebullient, the wrath is addressed less towards the people than towards the forces that fuel their dark deeds. In an elegant inversion, the dogs are granted the gift of human speech and reason, and with this they attack the dog-like or bestial nature of the humans they serve.

The reader familiar with *Don Quixote* will have encountered the conflict that dominates the work; a conflict between fact and fiction, truth and falsehood, and the word and its meaning. One principal source of this lies in the complexity of narrative layers within the two parts of the novel. In brief, the reader is introduced to the text by the author Cervantes. It is then continued by an unnamed narrator who had the work translated from the Arabic after finding the original by Cide Hamete in a marketplace in Toledo. The knight of the first part, indeed, performed his actions so that they would be written down; and yet before Cervantes published the second part, a certain Avellaneda had already published an alternative second part to the knight's adventures. Don Quixote himself is then aware of this text in Cervantes' work. Similar conflicts are apparent in this *novela*. Working outwards from the narrative of the witch, we read the speech of Montiela, narrated by Cañizares, overheard and later narrated by Berganza the dog, overheard and later written by Campuzano, read by Peralta, recorded by the narrator – with the figure of Cervantes surrounding the whole. In this lies the importance of the first tale encircling the second, as between the reader and the narrative of the dog appears another (fictitious) layer of readership. Returning to this model, as each narrative unfolds, incredulity or misinterpretation challenges the truth of the narration. The dog Berganza, prior to acquiring human reason, cannot be trusted to have interpreted the witch's monologue; the other dog, Scipio, then disbelieves its veracity. The incredulous Peralta then reads the text of an author (Campuzano) who claims to have heard dogs talk, who has been deeply ill, and has already admitted in his first narration to being deceitful. As each narrative layer unfolds, the pairs of narrators/ characters discuss the nature of truth and fiction, questioning to what degree one can be enlightened or deceived through belief or disbelief in the fiction. Consequently the reader and the author ultimately come together outside the work as the final layer in this complex structure.

This narrative complexity can then be linked to the constant concerns of appearance and reality and the word and its meaning that appear in both tales. Berganza highlights throughout his speech examples of positive appearances that disguise bad interiors, and noble and lofty words that disguise bad deeds. Berganza himself notes that while once in the past he urgently wanted to communicate, all he could do was bark. This provokes questions concerning the use of language and the use of fiction: the dogs have here been granted language, and they use it to communicate, educate, entertain and learn, whereas these dark, human characters use language to deceive. Indeed, the dogs discuss how they must rise above the base human sin of gossiping and slandering. Thus, just as for the knight Don Quixote his nag is a steed, a basin is a helmet, sheep are an army and windmills are giants, so within the dogs' colloquy the established connections between language and meaning are shown to be more shifting and unreliable than one may expect.

The reader is under no obligation to search for any *ejemplo* or meaning within any of the *novelas ejemplares*. However, were the reader to draw an evil lesson, says Cervantes in the prologue, he would cut off his hand – a weighty pledge considering that he had lost his left hand in the battle of Lepanto. Indeed, as stated earlier, both Cervantes and his characters always stress the need for entertainment. In this respect a variant semantic definition of the term *ejemplar* could be considered. Firstly, with the numerous debates about truth, fiction and the art of narration, both tales become 'examples' of the storyteller's art, wherein the craft of fiction is analysed. Secondly, with the richness of characterisation, the abundance of images, conversations, debates and adventures, the colloquy could be considered an 'example', or sample, of life. Just as in life meaning is never explicit and unanimous, so in this tale, where the fabric of fiction and reality, authorship and readership is questioned, meaning can never be simple and direct.

It is precisely in this absence of direct answers that the work of Cervantes will continue to be read and debated for generations. 'In the ambiguous time of art,' declares Borges, 'Hamlet is sane *and* is mad.' In the ambiguous world of Cervantes, readers are authors and authors readers, windmills are and are not giants, infants are and are not converted into dogs, and dogs do and do not speak.

–William Rowlandson, 2004

Note on the Text:
This translation is based on the Cátedra edition of *Las Novelas ejemplares*, 1995, ed. Harry Sieber, which itself follows the text of the first edition of Juan de la Cuesta, Madrid, 1613, published by the Real Academia Española, Madrid, 1917.

The Deceitful Marriage

A soldier was hobbling out of the Hospital of the Resurrection, which lies just outside the Puerta del Campo in Valladolid, using his sword as a walking stick. You could see by the weakness of his legs and by his yellow complexion that, although the weather was not particularly hot, he must have sweated out in twenty days all the fluids that he had probably absorbed in one hour. He stumbled and staggered like someone recovering from an illness, and as he passed through the city gate, he saw a friend of his coming towards him whom he had not seen for more than six months. The man crossed himself as if he had seen a ghost, and said as he approached him, 'What's this, Ensign Campuzano? Is it possible that you're in these lands? I could have sworn you were in Flanders wielding a pike and not here dragging a sword. Why are you looking so pale and so weak?'

To this Campuzano replied, 'As to whether I am in these lands or not, Licentiate Peralta, you're looking at the answer. To the rest of your questions I can say only that I've just come out of hospital after sweating out a dozen or so sores given to me by a woman whom I took to be mine when I shouldn't have done so.'

'So you were married then?'

'Indeed I was.'

'It must have been a passionate affair,' said Peralta, 'and marriages based on passion carry regret with them.'

'I can't say whether it was passionate,' replied the ensign, 'although I'll confirm that it was painful, for from my betrothal, or betrayal,[1] I got so many pains in body and soul that it took forty sweating treatments to cure the bodily ones, and as for the pains of the soul – well, I've found no cure. However, since I'm in no state to have long chats in the street, you'll have to forgive me until some other more convenient day. Then I'll give you the full account of these events that are likely to be the strangest and most extraordinary news that you'll have ever heard in all the days of your life.'

'No need to wait,' said the licentiate. 'Why not come and do penance with me at my lodgings? I have some stew, which they say is very good for you when you're ill, and although I've only enough for two, my servant will just have to make do with a bit of pie; and if that doesn't put you on the road to recovery, then a few slices of that excellent ham from Rute certainly will, coupled with my good intentions in offering it to you, not only now, but whenever you like.'

Campuzano thanked him, and accepted the invitation and the offer. They first went and heard Mass at the church of San Llorent, and then Peralta took him home, gave him what he had promised, offered him more and, when they had finished eating, asked him to recount the events that he had so boasted about. Campuzano didn't have to be asked twice, and immediately began to speak as follows:

'You'll no doubt remember, Licentiate Peralta, how here in this city I was teamed up with Captain Pedro de Herrera, who's now away in Flanders?'

'Yes, I remember well,' replied Peralta.

'Well,' continued Campuzano, 'one particular day, we had just finished eating at that inn called La Solana, which was also where we were staying, when two charming-looking ladies came in, accompanied by their two maids. One of the women leant against the window with the captain and began to chat with him, while the other sat down on the chair next to me, with her shawl pulled down all the way to her chin, so that all one could see of her face was what the fine texture of the material revealed. Although I begged her to be so kind as to reveal her face, it was impossible to persuade her to do so, and this I found only inflamed my desire to see her. And then, whether by accident or design I don't know, she increased my desire even more by revealing a pearl-white hand, adorned with wonderful rings. Well, in those days I myself was rather dapper, with that large chain that you surely remember, a large hat with feather and hatband, a colourful uniform, all befitting a soldier; and so splendid did I, in my delusion, consider myself, that I believed I could have any woman I desired. In that frame of mind, I asked her to lift the shawl and show her face. She replied to me:

'"Do not press me so. I have a house; have a servant follow me there, for, although I am more respectable than this response implies, if I see that you are as discreet as you are dashing, I shall be pleased to welcome you there."

'I kissed her hands in thanks for the great favour she was doing me, in return for which I promised her vast amounts of gold. The

4

captain finished his conversation, the women left, and a servant of mine followed them. The captain then told me that what the woman wanted him to do was to take some letters to Flanders for another captain who she said was her cousin, although he knew she was talking about her lover. I was spellbound by the snow-white hands that I had seen, and enraptured by the face that I desired to see; and so the following day, guided there by my servant, I was admitted into her house. I found a well-kept house and a woman of nearly thirty whom I recognised by her hands. She was not outstandingly beautiful, but she charmed me when she spoke, with a tone of voice so sweet that it went from my ears straight to my very soul. I had long, amorous conversations with her; I bragged, I boasted, I exaggerated, I made offers, I made promises, and said all that I thought would be needed to win her affection. However, as she appeared accustomed to hearing similar or even better offers, it seemed that she listened to me more out of politeness than credulity. In the end, we kept up this idle chat for four days, without me managing to seize the fruit that I so desired.

'In the times that I visited her, I always found the house empty and never caught sight of either imaginary relatives or real friends; although she did have a servant girl, who was more crafty than simple. In the end, treating my passion like that of a soldier on the eve of departing, I put some pressure on my lady Doña Estefanía de Caicedo (for that was the name of the woman who had won my heart), and she replied to me:

'"My dear Ensign Campuzano, it would be foolish of me to try to pass myself off to you as a saint. I have been, and even am now, a sinner, but not so that the neighbours gossip about me, nor strangers notice me. From neither my parents nor any relatives have I inherited any wealth, and yet despite this my entire household is worth some two thousand five hundred escudos, and all this in things that would take no time converting to money at auction. With this wealth I am looking for a husband to devote myself to and to obey, and, besides mending my ways, I will pamper him and serve him. No prince has a cook who can make more tasty dishes or give those special touches to stews than I can when, wanting to be domestic, I put my mind to it. I can be the house butler, the kitchen maid and the lady in the drawing room. In brief, I know how to give orders and make myself obeyed. I never waste anything and I save a great deal; my money is worth more, and not less, when it is spent as I decree. All the linen of the house, which is plentiful and of excellent quality, does not come from shops or drapers, but was sewn by these very fingers and those of my servants; and if the cloth could have been woven at home, then it would have been. I sing my praises so highly not through arrogance, but through the necessity of doing so. Finally, I want to say that I'm looking for a husband who will protect me, rule me and honour me, and not some lover who will serve me and then insult me. If you accept the pledge and the treasure that are offered, here I am, plain and honest before you, willing to agree with anything you may decide, and without putting myself on the market, which is the same as putting myself in the hands of matchmakers, for no one is better at arranging affairs than the involved parties themselves."

'Well, at that stage my judgement was clearly in my heels and not in my head, making pleasure seem far greater than anything my imagination could offer, and offering before my eyes such a wealth of property that I could already see it converted into money. The only argument I listened to was dictated by my pleasure, and my pleasure had suffocated my reason. I told her that I was the luckiest man alive, because Heaven had bestowed, as if by miracle, such a companion as her to be mistress of my will and my possessions. These were by no means inconsiderable, taking into account the chain I wore around my neck and the other jewels I kept at home, which, together with the possibility of selling off some of my soldier's finery, would amount to more than two thousand ducats. All this, combined with the two and a half thousand of hers, would be sufficient for us to go off and live in comfort in the village where I was born and where I had roots. This property, bolstered with the money and by selling the fruit in season, could provide us with a happy and peaceful life.

'And so, there and then we decided to get married, and we arranged the proof that we were single, the marriage banns were read on three consecutive holy days, and on the fourth day we were married. Two friends of mine were present at the wedding, along with a youth who she said was her cousin, whom I accepted as a relative with the kindest of words, just as were all my words that I had so far said to my new wife, despite – and here I wish to remain silent – my twisted and devious intentions. For, although I am telling the truth, they are not, I'm afraid, the truths of the confessional.

'My servant moved my trunk from the inn where I was staying to my wife's house, and in her presence I locked away my magnificent chain. I showed her another three or four chains which, if not so big, were of better craftsmanship, along with three or four hatbands of different styles. I showed off to her my fine uniform and the feathers, and I handed over to her almost four hundred *reales* for the household expenses. For six days I enjoyed the first fruits of marriage, relaxing in the house like the penniless fellow at the house of his rich father-in-law. I walked on lush carpets, I crumpled linen sheets from Holland, and lit my way with silver candlesticks. I ate my breakfast in bed, rose at eleven, took lunch at twelve, and at two slept a siesta in the drawing room. Doña Estefanía and the servant girl waited on me hand and foot. Moreover my servant, whom I had always considered a lazy and slothful fellow, had become as lively and sprightly as a deer. In those moments that Doña Estefanía was not at my side, she would be found in the kitchen, diligently preparing dishes that would awaken my taste buds and sharpen my appetite. My shirts, collars and handkerchiefs smelt like the city of Aranjuez in bloom, scented with the perfumed water and orange blossom that she scattered on them.

'Those days flew past, as do the years governed by the laws of time; and during those days, seeing myself so well looked after and cared for, the bad intentions with which that affair had begun gradually started to transform into good ones.

'At length a morning came when there was a loud pounding at the street door. The maid leant out of the window, but brought her head back in quickly, saying:

'"Oh, what a time for her to turn up. Didn't she write the other day that she would be here much later?"

'"Well, who is it who has arrived?" I asked the girl.

'"Who?" she replied. "None other than my lady Doña Clementa Bueso, accompanied by Don Lope Meléndez de Almendáraz and two

7

servants, and Hortigosa, the lady-in-waiting she took with her."

'"Well, hurry up, girl, for heaven's sake, and let them in!" Doña Estefanía said at this point. "And you, sir, in honour of my love do not be alarmed, nor yet respond on my behalf to anything that you may hear against me."

'"But, who is there who might say anything against you, especially in front of me? Tell me, who are these people whose arrival has upset you so much?"

'"Now is not the time to tell you," said Doña Estefanía. "Only you must know that everything that happens here is a pretence whose aim and purpose will become clear to you in time."

'Although I wanted to reply to this, Doña Clementa Bueso did not give me the chance, for she entered the room, dressed in lustrous green satin with much gold braid, a cape of the same design with the same trim, a hat with green, white and red feathers and a rich gold band, and a fine veil which covered half her face. With her came Don Lope Meléndez de Almendáraz, no less elegant and dressed sumptuously for travelling. Hortigosa was the first to speak:

'"Heavens! What is this? My lady Doña Clementa's bed is occupied, and what's more, occupied by a man. I must be seeing things in this house today! I'll swear that Doña Estefanía has overstepped the mark this time, and has taken advantage of my lady's friendship."

'"I agree entirely with what you say, Hortigosa," replied Doña Clementa, "but the fault is mine. When will I learn not to have friends who are only friends when it is to their advantage?"

'To all this Doña Estefanía answered:

'"Please do not be upset, my lady Doña Clementa Bueso, and please understand that to all this mystery that you see in this house there is an explanation. When you know the truth, I know that I will be forgiven and that you will have no cause for complaint."

'By this stage I had already put on my breeches and doublet, and Doña Estefanía took me by the hand and led me to another room, where she told me that her friend wanted to play a trick on Don Lope, who had come with her, and whom she planned to marry; and that the trick was to make him think that the house and everything in it belonged to her, and that she was intending to give it all to him as a dowry. Her plan was that after the marriage she didn't care if the deception was discovered, as she was confident of Don Lope's deep love for her.

'"And then afterwards my property shall be returned to me, and no one will hold it against her, nor indeed against any other woman who tries to find an honourable husband even through trickery."

'I replied that she was stretching friendship to its limits with these actions, and that she should first think the whole matter over very carefully, as later she may well have to go to court to get her property back. But she responded with so many reasons, listing the many ways in which she was indebted to Doña Clementa, which obliged her to help her out even in matters of greatest importance, and that, despite my suspicions and better judgement, I simply had to go along with the whims of Doña Estefanía. She assured me that the deception game would be over within eight days, and in the meantime we were to stay at the house of another of her friends. She and I finished dressing, and then, after she had gone in to take leave of Doña Clementa Bueso and Don Lope Meléndez de Almendáraz, she ordered my servant to pick up my trunk and to follow her. I also followed her without having taken my leave of anyone.

'Doña Estefanía stopped at the house of a friend of hers, but before we went in she spent a long while speaking to her. Finally a maid came out and said that my servant and I should enter. She led us to a narrow room in which there were two beds so close together that, seeing as there was no space to separate them, they looked like one bed, with the sheets of both touching each other. In the event we were there for six days, and in all of them not a day passed that we didn't quarrel. I kept telling her how stupid she had been to lend her house and property, even if it were to her own mother.

'Well, I kept this up to such a degree that one day, when Doña Estefanía had said that she would go and see how the business had turned out, the lady of the house asked me why it was that I criticised her so harshly, and what it was that she had done that I kept calling an act of utmost stupidity and not an act of pure friendship.

'I told her the entire story, and when I reached the point at which

I married Doña Estefanía, and the dowry that she had brought, and her foolishness in leaving her house and belongings to Doña Clementa – even though it was with the noble intention of securing such a suitable husband as Don Lope – the lady crossed herself rapidly and repeated, "Oh, my God, what a wicked woman", again and again. This put me in a state of terrible anxiety, but she finally said:

'"Señor Ensign, I don't know if I'm acting against my conscience in revealing to you something that would weigh on my conscience if I didn't tell you. But my faith is with God and Fortune. For truth, and may falsehood be damned! Well, the honest truth is that Doña Clementa is the real lady of the house and property that was given to you as a dowry. Everything that Doña Estefanía has told you has been a lie; for she owns neither house, nor property, nor any other dress other than what she's wearing. The reason she was able to play this trick was because Doña Clementa had gone to stay with some relatives of hers in the city of Plasencia, and from there she went for the nine-day prayers at the convent of Our Lady of Guadalupe. During this period she left her house to Doña Estefanía, so that she might look after it. They're good friends, you see. Although at the end of the day who can blame Doña Estefanía for what she's done, for she has been able to secure herself such a fine husband as yourself, Señor Ensign."

'Here she ended her speech, and I was beginning to despair, and no doubt I would have done so if my guardian angel had not interceded to help me, for he came to tell me to remember in my heart that I was a Christian, and that the worst sin a man can suffer is despair, as it is the sin of the devil. This consideration, or inspiration, comforted me somewhat, but not so much that it prevented me grabbing my cape and sword and rushing out to look for Doña Estefanía, with the intention of dealing her an exemplary punishment. However, Fate, for better or for worse, decreed that I was unable to find Doña Estefanía in any of the places I sought her. I went to San Llorent, commended myself to Our Lady, sat down in a pew, and in my sorrow I fell into such a deep sleep that I would have slept for days had I not been awakened.

'With a troubled and brooding mind I went to the house of Doña

Clementa, whom I found perfectly at ease and relaxed as the rightful lady of the house. I didn't dare say anything to her of the matter as Don Lope was there, and so I returned to the house of my hostess. She told me that she had told Doña Estefanía that I knew all about her tricks and deceits, that Doña Estefanía had asked her what my reaction had been to such news, and that she had replied very bad, and that in her opinion I had left the house in a terrible frame of mind, and with a fierce determination to find her. She told me, finally, that Doña Estefanía had carried off everything that was in the trunk, leaving me nothing but a set of travelling clothes.

'Well, if that wasn't the limit, I tell you. Once again I found myself at the mercy of the Almighty. I went to look at the trunk, and sure enough I found it yawning open like a tomb awaiting a corpse, which might well have been my own, had I had the sense to comprehend and take in the extent of my misfortune.'

'It was indeed a terrible misfortune,' interjected the Licentiate Peralta at this point, 'that Doña Estefanía carried off so many chains and hatbands. But, as they say, it never rains but it pours.'

'Well, the loss itself didn't upset me too much,' replied the ensign, 'for I myself can also say, "Don Simueque thought he was deceiving me with his squinting daughter, but, by God, I'm lopsided myself."'

'I'm not quite sure what you mean by that,' replied Peralta.

'The point is,' answered the ensign, 'that the entire hoard of chains, hatbands and trinkets could only have been worth around ten or twelve ducats.'

'But that's not possible,' replied the licentiate, 'because that chain that you used to wear around your neck certainly appeared to be worth more than two hundred ducats.'

'That would be the case,' said the ensign, 'if truth corresponded to appearance. But seeing that all that glitters is not gold, the chains, hatbands, jewels and trinkets were all only real in their artifice; but they were so well made that only fire or a thorough investigation would have revealed their falseness.'

'In which case,' declared the licentiate, 'it is all square between you and Doña Estefanía.'

'It is indeed,' replied the ensign, 'and such that we can now start from scratch. But the trouble is, Señor Licentiate, she can now dispose of my chains, but I cannot be rid of the deceit of her conduct. The fact is, whether I like it or not, the forfeit is mine.'

'Well, give thanks to God, Señor Campuzano, that your forfeit had legs, and has run off and left you, and that you don't have to go looking for it,' said Peralta.

'True, true,' replied the ensign. 'However, despite all this and without me looking for it, I find it always in my mind, and, wherever I go, I find my disgrace always present.'

'I don't know what to say to help you,' said Peralta, 'other than to remind you of a couple of verses of Petrarch that go:

Ché chi prende diletto di far frode;
Non si de lamentar s'altri l'inganna

which in our language means: "He who is in the habit of deceiving others should not complain when he himself is deceived."'

'I'm not complaining,' replied the ensign, 'but I feel sorry for myself, for the guilty man does not stop feeling the pain of his punishment just because he recognises his guilt. I see very well that I set out to deceive, and was deceived myself, because I became entangled in my own net, but I cannot control my feelings so well that I do not feel sorry for myself. Finally, to come to the main point of my story (for certainly all that happened to me could be called a story), I found out that Doña Estefanía had been taken away by the cousin who, I told you, attended our wedding, and who had been her companion for a long while. But I had no desire to go looking for her, so as not to fall into any further trouble. Within a few days I not only changed my lodgings, but changed my hair, because my eyebrows and eyelashes had begun to fall out, and, gradually, all my hair began to fall out, and I became bald before my time, all due to a complaint known as "alopecia", or more commonly, "hair loss". I felt utterly stripped, as I had neither beard to comb nor money to spend. Added to this the illness progressed at the rate of my growing needs, for poverty kills honour, leading some to the gallows, others to the hospital, and others to enter their enemies' houses, begging and pleading, which is surely the greatest misfortune a man down on his luck can suffer. So as not to have to pay for treatment by selling my clothes, which were to be my only means to keep my honour once my health was restored, when the time came that they offered sweating treatments at the Hospital of the Resurrection, I went in, where I undertook forty sweating sessions. They say I'll stay well if I look after myself. I have a sword, and the rest, well, it's in the hands of God.'

The licentiate offered his assistance once again, astonished at the things he had been told.

'It appears that it doesn't take much to astonish you, Señor Peralta,' said the ensign, 'for you see there are still more things for me to recount that exceed all imagination, as they go beyond the bounds of nature. Suffice it to say that all my misfortunes up to this point have been of great value to me, as it was thanks to them that I ended up in the hospital where I was witness to what I'm now going to tell you, and which neither you, nor anyone alive on earth, will ever believe.'

All these rambles and preambles that the ensign made before telling the story inflamed the interest and curiosity of Peralta so much that he begged him, without further ado, to begin the tale.

'You will have noticed,' said the ensign, 'two dogs with lanterns that stroll at night with the friars of Capacha, lighting them when they beg for alms?'

'Yes, I've seen them,' replied Peralta.

'You'll have also seen, or heard,' continued the ensign, 'what is said about them: that if by chance anyone throws alms from a window which fall on the ground – well – these dogs run up to light up the spot and to look for what has fallen. They also stop in front of windows where they know that people often give them alms, and although in this they are so gentle that they appear more like lambs than dogs, in the hospital they are a couple of lions, guarding the house with great care and vigilance.'

'Yes, I've heard of all that,' said Peralta, 'but there's no reason why that should astonish me.'

'Well, what I'm going to tell you now about them certainly will astonish you, and without crossing yourself and claiming that it is impossible or improbable, prepare yourself to believe it. The truth is,

I heard and as good as saw with my own eyes these two dogs, the one called Scipio and the other Berganza. It was at night (the penultimate night of my sweating treatment), I was stretched out behind my bed on some old mats, and in the middle of the night, as I was lying awake in the dark, thinking about my past life and my present misfortunes, I heard voices talking together nearby. I listened attentively to see if I could work out who was speaking and what they were talking about, and, in a short while, I came to realise from what they were saying that the owners of these voices were none other than the two dogs Scipio and Berganza.'

No sooner had Campuzano uttered these words than the licentiate, standing up, said:

'May God grant you the very best of luck, my dear Señor Campuzano, for up to now I was in doubt as to whether to believe or not all that you had told me about your marriage. But what you've started telling me now about hearing two dogs talk has utterly convinced me that I shouldn't believe a word you say. For the love of God, Ensign, don't tell these fairy stories to anyone else, unless it's someone who is as close a friend of yours as I am.'

'Don't think me so ignorant,' replied Campuzano, 'that I'm not fully aware that animals do not talk except in a miracle. For I know full well that if thrushes, magpies and parrots do indeed talk, it's no more than with words that they pick up and memorise, and because they have a tongue suitable for pronouncing them. But this does not enable these birds to speak and reply in intelligent discourse, as these dogs did. Of course, many times since I heard them, I've thought that maybe I imagined it all. I've wanted to believe that I was dreaming all that which, with my God-given five senses awake and alert, I heard, listened to, noted and finally wrote down without missing a single word; all of which should be enough proof to persuade and convince you that I am telling the truth. The subjects the dogs dealt with were many and varied, more akin to the conversation of wise men than of mere dogs; and so, since I couldn't have made it up myself, despite everything and against my better judgement, I've come to the conclusion that I was not dreaming and that the dogs really were talking.'

'Good grief!' replied the licentiate, 'we're back in those mythical and fantastical days of Maricastaña, where pumpkins talked; or maybe we're in one of Aesop's tales, where the cockerel chatted with the fox and all the animals talked to each other.'

'One such animal, and certainly the greatest, would be me,' replied the ensign, 'if I believed that those days had returned. But then so would I be one if I stopped believing what I heard and what I saw and what I'll dare to swear with an oath that would oblige and even force Incredulity herself to believe it. And just assuming that I've been mistaken, and that my truth is mere fantasy, and that insisting on it is folly, would you not enjoy, Señor Peralta, to see written down in a colloquy the things that these dogs, or whoever they were, talked about?'

'As long as you don't exhaust yourself in attempting to convince me that you heard the dogs talk, I'll gladly listen to the dialogue, which, as it is written down and noted by the talent of the ensign himself, I already judge to be good.'

'Well, there is one more thing,' said the ensign. 'Seeing that I was so attentive, that my judgement was refined, and my memory so sharp, lucid and unburdened (thanks to the many raisins and almonds I had eaten), I ascribed the whole dialogue to memory, and the following day I wrote it all down, without seeking colourful rhetoric to adorn it, and without adding or removing any detail to make it more pleasing. The dialogue did not take place on just one, but two consecutive nights, although I have written down just the first night, which is the life of Berganza. The story of Scipio (the subject of the second night) I intend to write when I see that this first tale is, if not believed, then at least not scorned. I have the dialogue here on my person at present; I wrote it in the form of a colloquy in order to avoid having to state, "said Scipio… Berganza replied", which tends to lengthen the writing.'

Saying this, he took from his shirt a notebook and put it in the hands of the licentiate, who took it and laughed as though he were making fun of all that he had heard and expected to read.

'I'll just sit back in this chair,' said the ensign, 'while you read, if you wish, those dreams and absurdities, which have no other merit than that you can stop reading them if they get tiresome.'

'You do as you please,' said Peralta, 'for this dialogue will not take me very long to get through.'

The ensign sat back, the licentiate opened the notebook, and at the top he saw that it bore the following title:

The story and dialogue which took place between Scipioand Berganza, dogs of the Hospital of the Resurrection, which is in the city of Valladolid, outside the Puerta del Campo, and who are commonly known as Mahudes' dogs.

The Dialogue of the Dogs

SCIPIO: My dear friend Berganza, let us tonight leave the hospital to be guarded by good faith, and let us retire to the peace and quiet amongst these mats, where we can enjoy, without being disturbed, this miraculous gift that Heaven has granted us both in the same instant.

BERGANZA: Scipio, my brother, I can hear you speak, and I know that I am speaking to you, and yet I cannot believe it, for it seems to me that for us to speak defies the laws of nature.

SCIPIO: Very true, Berganza, and this miracle is even more prodigious considering that not only do we speak, but we also speak in intelligent discourse, as if we had the power of reason, despite the fact that we cannot have reason as the difference between man and beast is that man is a rational being and the beast irrational.

BERGANZA: I understand everything you say, Scipio, and the fact that you say it and that I understand it causes me further wonder and astonishment. It is true that on many occasions throughout the course of my life I have heard talk of our superior qualities; so much, indeed, that it appears that some people have believed that we have a natural instinct, so keen and sharp in so many ways, that it points to the idea that we possess some degree of understanding capable of intelligent discourse.

SCIPIO: What I have heard praised and extolled is our prodigious memory, our gratitude and our fidelity; so much that we are generally portrayed as a symbol of friendship. Thus you will have seen (if you've ever considered it) that on those alabaster tombs which usually have effigies of those buried beneath, if it should be a man and wife, they always place between them at their feet the figure of a dog, as a sign that during their lifetime they preserved an inviolable friendship and fidelity to each other.

BERGANZA: I know for a fact that there have been some dogs so loyal that they have thrown themselves into the same grave with the dead bodies of their masters. Others have stationed themselves upon the tombs where their masters are buried, never leaving, nor eating, until they themselves passed away. I know likewise that, after the elephant, the dog apparently holds first place for wisdom and understanding, followed by the horse, and lastly the ape.

Scipio: Very true. However you must admit that you've neither seen nor heard mention of any elephant, dog, horse or monkey that has ever spoken. Because of this I deduce that our sudden and unexpected gift of speech may be classed amongst those things called portents – which, as is proved by experience, appear when some great calamity threatens people.

Berganza: Well, if that is the case then I will certainly take as a portentous sign what I heard a student say the other day, passing through Alcalá de Henares.

Scipio: What did you hear him say?

Berganza: He said that of the five thousand students studying at the university that year, two thousand were reading medicine.

Scipio: Well, what do you infer from that?

Berganza: I infer that either these two thousand doctors will have patients to cure (which would mean a terrible plague and great misfortune), or that they will all die of hunger.

Scipio: Well, whatever it may mean, portent or not, you and I are speaking. Let whatever Heaven has ordained happen, for neither diligence nor human wisdom can prevent it. Therefore there is no reason for us to question how and why we can talk, instead let us make hay while the sun, or in this case the moon, shines. It's comfortable here amongst these mats, we have no idea how long this good fortune will last, and so let us make the most of it and talk all through the night, without giving in to sleep, which would rob us of this pleasure that I have so longed for.

Berganza: I too, ever since I had the strength to gnaw a bone, have had the desire to speak, in order to utter those things that had accumulated in my memory. For so long had those myriad thoughts settled there that they had grown mouldy or had disappeared altogether. Now, however, seeing that I am suddenly and unexpectedly enriched with this divine gift of speech, I intend to enjoy it and take full advantage of it, hastening me to say everything that I can recall all at once, even though it may come out muddled and confused, as I have no idea when I'll be asked to hand back this gift, which, I fear, is only on loan.

Scipio: Well, let's make that our plan, Berganza, my friend: that tonight you tell me the story of your life and the perils that have led you to the point in which you find yourself now, and that if tomorrow night we still find ourselves gifted with speech, I'll tell you my life story; for it will be far better to spend our time telling our own life stories than trying to find out about other people's.

BERGANZA: I have always, Scipio, taken you for a dear, wise and sensible friend, now more than ever, since as a friend you want to hear about my life and tell me about yours, and as wise you have divided the time in order for us to do so. But first make absolutely sure that no one is listening to us.

SCIPIO: As far as I can tell there's no one, for although there is a soldier nearby undergoing a sweat treatment, at this hour he'll be more inclined to sleep than to go eavesdropping on anyone.

BERGANZA: Well, then, if I can speak with that assurance, listen; and if what I'm telling you bores or tires you, either tell me so, or ask me to be silent.

SCIPIO: Speak until first light, or until someone hears us. I'll very willingly listen to you and will not interrupt you unless I deem it necessary.

BERGANZA: I believe that I saw the light of day for the first time in Seville, in its main abattoir, which lies just outside the Puerta de la Carne². From this I imagine (were it not for what I'll tell you later) that my parents must have been mastiffs of the type that are bred by those lords of chaos and confusion otherwise known as butchers. The first master I had was called Nicolás el Romo, a swarthy fellow, stocky and hot-tempered, just like all those who wield knives in slaughterhouses. This fellow Nicolás taught me and some other pups, in the company of some older mastiffs, to charge at the bulls and take hold of their ears. In no time at all I became an expert in this.

SCIPIO: That doesn't surprise me in the least, Berganza, for we are naturally prone to do wrong, and therefore we quickly learn to practise it.

BERGANZA: What I could tell you, Scipio, my brother, of the things I saw in that slaughterhouse, and of the extraordinary things that went on in there! The first thing you must realise is that all those who work there, from the lowest to the highest, are people of limited conscience, without pity or mercy, with no fear of the King or his justice; and most of them have some girl on the side. They are like bloodthirsty birds of prey, keeping both themselves and their girlfriends with what they steal. Before dawn on the days when meat arrives, a large crowd of young men and women gathers at the slaughterhouse, carrying empty sacks which they fill with bits of meat, while the maids go off with sweetbreads and almost whole sides of meat. No animal is slaughtered without these people carrying off their tithes and the best and most succulent morsels; and seeing that in Seville there is no single official supplier of meat, everyone can bring whatever they choose, and the first beast to be slaughtered is either the best or the cheapest, and under this state of affairs there is always an abundance. The owners entrust themselves to these good people not so that they won't steal from them (that would be impossible to avoid), but so that they do not help themselves too freely to the slices and perks that they make of the slaughtered beasts, which they trim and prune as if they were willows or vines. But nothing horrified me more than to see these slaughterers kill a man with the same ease with which they would kill a cow. For a mere trifle, and quick as a flash, they would thrust a knife to the hilt into the belly of a man as if they were dispatching a bull. Only by a miracle could a day pass without a fight or a wounding, or at times a killing. They all rate themselves as brave and valiant men, although in truth there's more of the thug about them, and there isn't one amongst them who doesn't have his guardian angel, paid for by sides of meat and ox-tongues, in the Plaza de San Francisco. Finally, I heard a certain shrewd fellow say that the King still has three things to get under control in Seville: the Calle de la Caza, the Costanilla, and the slaughterhouse.

SCIPIO: My dear friend Berganza, if you're going to spend as long as you've just spent in recounting the particulars of each master that you've had and the faults of their profession, we'll have to appeal to Heaven to grant us the power of speech for at least a year, and even then I fear that, at the rate you're going, you'll only get halfway through your tale. And I'd like to point something out to you, the truth of which you'll notice when I tell you my own life story, and that is that in some stories, the appeal lies in the stories themselves, while in others the appeal lies in the way they are told. What I mean is that there are some stories that give pleasure even if they are told with neither preambles nor adornments, and there are others that require being dressed up in elegant words, and accompanied by facial expressions and hand gestures; and with hushing the voice, something grand is made out of something little; and from being dull and insipid the stories become witty and entertaining. Don't forget this point, and let it be at the forefront of your mind for the remainder of what you have to tell.

BERGANZA: I shall indeed do so, if I am able, and if the powerful urge to talk allows me to, although I think it'll be tremendously hard to keep myself under control.

SCIPIO: Control your tongue. For the tongue is the greatest cause of human misfortune.

BERGANZA: I shall explain, then, how my master taught me to carry a basket in my mouth, and how to defend it against anyone who may have tried to snatch it from me. He also showed me the house of his girlfriend, and thereby excused her maid from having to come to the slaughterhouse, for I brought to her in the early mornings all that he had pilfered during the night. And one day at dawn, as I was dutifully off on my way to deliver her share, I heard my name called out from a window. I looked up and saw the loveliest young girl. Well, I slowed a little, and she came down to the front door and called me once again. I went up to her, as if wanting to know what she wanted of me, and it turned out that it was no more than to take from me what I was carrying in the basket, and to replace it with an old sandal. Then I said to myself, 'The flesh returns to the flesh,' and the girl, having robbed me of the meat, said to me, 'Off you trot, Gavilán, or whatever your name is, and tell your master, Nicolás el Romo, not to place his trust in animals, and tell him never to expect gifts from the wolf.' I could easily have taken back what she had stolen from me; but I chose not to, so as not to put my dirty slaughterhouse mouth on those clean, white hands.

Scipio: You did well, for it is beauty's prerogative to be always respected.

Berganza: A respect which I observed; and thus, I returned to my master without the rations but with the sandal. It seemed to him that I had returned early, he saw the sandal, imagined the trick that had been played, took out a knife and made a thrust at me which, had I not jumped out of the way, you would not be hearing this tale now, nor the many others I intend to tell you. Taking to my heels, I immediately fled from San Bernardo[3], heading off into the unknown, wherever Fortune decided to take me. That night I slept under the stars, and the following day I had the good fortune to run into a flock or herd of sheep and lambs. As soon as I saw the flock, I thought that I had found the true essence of my happiness and ease, as it seemed to me the most natural and proper occupation for dogs to look after livestock. It is a work of great virtue as it consists in protecting and defending the humble and weak from the proud and powerful. No sooner had one of the three shepherds tending to the flock seen me than he called out to me, 'Here, boy!' and I, who desired nothing more than this, went up to him, lowering my head and wagging my tail. He ran his hand over my back, opened my mouth, spat in it, examined my fangs, guessed at my age, and said to the other shepherds that I had all the marks of a dog of good breeding.

At that moment the chief stockman rode up on a grey mare, using short stirrups, carrying a lance and shield, and looking withal more the coastal warden than the sheep farmer. He asked the shepherd:

'Where did this dog come from? He's got the signs of being a good one.'

'You can be sure of that,' replied the shepherd, 'for I have examined him closely, and there is no indication that he won't turn out to be a great dog. He just pitched up here; I've no idea whose dog he is, but I do know that he's not from any flock in these parts.'

'Since that is so,' replied the owner, 'give him the collar of Leoncillo, the dog that died, give him the same food as the rest, and pamper him a little, so that he takes a liking to the flock and stays with it.'

Upon saying this he left, and the shepherd put around my neck a strong collar with steel studs, having first given me a bowl of bread and milk. Likewise he named me Barcino. I was overjoyed with my second master and my new job; I showed myself to be attentive and careful in watching the flock, never leaving it, aside from during my siesta which I would spend either in the shade of some tree or of some river-bed or rock, or of some bush at the banks of one of the many streams that flowed around there. And even those hours of rest were not wasted away lazily, for I spent them exercising my memory in recalling many things, especially the life that I had spent in the slaughterhouse, and in the life that my master and all those like him had led, slaves to the whims and desires of their women. Oh, how many things I could tell you now about what I learnt in the school of my master's lady at the slaughterhouse. But I'll have to keep quiet about them, lest you call me a long-winded gossip and a slanderer.

SCIPIO: I've heard it said that a great poet of ancient times declared that it was difficult not to write satires, so I will allow you to gossip a little, but to illuminate and not to harm. What I mean is that you point, but that you don't wound or kill anyone in what you point out. Gossip, although it may make people laugh, is not a good thing if it kills; and if you can entertain without it, I shall consider you the height of wisdom.

BERGANZA: I shall take your advice, and I shall eagerly await the time that you tell me your story. From someone who can so well detect and remedy the defects that I have in telling my story, one may expect that he will tell his own story in a manner that instructs and delights at the same time. However, picking up the broken thread of my own tale, I'll tell you that in the solitude and silence of those siestas, amongst other things, I reckoned that what I had heard said about the life of shepherds could not possibly be true, at least, what I had heard about the lives that my master's girlfriend had read about in books when I went to her house. These books all told of shepherds and shepherdesses, how they spent their entire lives singing and playing the bagpipes, the pan pipes, the lute and the flute, and other extraordinary instruments. I would stop what I was doing to listen to her read of how the shepherd Anfriso sang sweetly and divinely in praise of the peerless Belisarda, and how there was not a single tree trunk in all the hills of Arcadia where he did not sit and sing, from the rising of the sun in the arms of Aurora, to the setting of the sun in the arms of Thetis; and even after Black Night had spread her dark and shadowy wings across the face of the land, still he did not cease his well-sung and well-cried laments. Nor did she fail to read about the shepherd Elicio, more amorous than valiant, of whom it was said that, neglectful both of his loves and his flock, he was ever attentive to the troubles of other people. She also spoke about how the great shepherd Fílida, the painter of a fine portrait, had been more trusted than fortunate. She said that she gave thanks to God for reading about the swoons of Sireno, the remorse of Diana, and the wise Felicia, who, with her enchanted water, untied that tangled web and unravelled that twisted maze of difficulties.[4] I recalled many other books of this type that I had heard her read, but they were not worthy of being brought to mind.

SCIPIO: You're certainly following my advice, Berganza, you lash the tongue, sting and move on; and let your intention be pure, even if your tongue appears not to be.

BERGANZA: In these matters, the tongue never stumbles if the intention does not fall first, but if by chance through carelessness or malice I do slander anyone, I shall respond to whoever criticises me in the same way that Mauleón[5], daft poet and laughable academic of the Academy of Imitators, responded to someone who asked him what was meant by the phrase *Deum de deo*[6], and he replied, 'Do as you desire'.

SCIPIO: Well, that's the response of a simpleton; but you, if you are indeed wise, or wish to be so, you'd do well never to say anything for which you must apologise. Pray continue.

BERGANZA: Well, then, all these reflections of mine that I've talked about, and many more, made me see how the various customs and practices of my shepherds and all the others of that coastal region differed from those shepherds that I'd heard about from those pastoral books. You see, if mine sang, their songs were certainly not tuneful or well composed, but more like '*Look out for the wolf, Juanica*', and others of that sort, and certainly not sung to the strains of the flute, the lute and the bagpipe, but to the sound of knocking two crooks together, or the clicking of bits of tile between finger and thumb. Similarly, there were no delicate, harmonious and admirable voices, but harsh throaty voices which, either solo or together, appeared not so much like singing but shouting, or even grunting. They spent most of the day either picking off their fleas or mending their sandals, nor were any of them named Amarillis, Fílida, Galatea or Diana, nor Lisardo, Lauso, Jacinto or Riselo; they all bore names like Antón, Domingo, Pablo or Llorente, from which I understood what I believe everyone must believe – namely, that those books are well-written pieces of fancy for the entertainment of the idle, and have no truth in them whatsoever. Were they to have an ounce of truth, then surely amongst my shepherds there would have been at least some relic of that most blissful of lives, of those lush meadows, leafy forests, sacred mountains, delightful gardens, clear streams and crystal springs, of those pure and sweetly delivered love verses, and of the shepherd who faints here, the shepherdess who swoons there, the flute resounding over here, and the pipes a-piping over there.

SCIPIO: Enough, Berganza, return to your path and proceed.

BERGANZA: Thank you, Scipio, my friend, for if you hadn't warned me – well, my tongue would have loosened so much that I wouldn't have drawn breath until I'd portrayed for you an entire book of this type that deceived me. But there will be a time in which I tell everything more coherently and in a better language than now.

SCIPIO: Look down at your feet, and that'll bring you back to earth, Berganza. What I mean is that you are an animal who lacks reason, and that if at the moment you appear to have some, the two of us have already established that it's something unprecedented and supernatural.

BERGANZA: That would indeed be so, if I were still in my first innocence, but now that I've remembered what it was that I should have said at the beginning of our conversation, not only am I amazed at what I am saying, but I am appalled at what I'm leaving out.

SCIPIO: Well, then, are you not going to tell me what it is that you've just remembered?

BERGANZA: It concerns a certain adventure that took place between me and a great sorceress, a disciple of Camacha de Montilla.

SCIPIO: Before continuing with the rest of your life story, do please tell me about this.

BERGANZA: I certainly shall not recount it now, not until its proper time. Be patient and listen to these events in their order, for in this way they'll give you more pleasure, unless you tend to get bored by wanting to hear the middle before the beginning.

SCIPIO: Be brief, then, and say what you will and how you will.

BERGANZA: Very well, what I'll say is that I felt very happy in my role of guarding the flock, for I felt that I was earning my bread by the sweat of my brow and by my labour, and that idleness, the mother of all vices, had nothing whatsoever to do with me, for if some days I rested, I did not sleep by night, for the wolves often attacked us and spurred us to arms. No sooner did I hear the shepherds holler, 'Get the wolf, Barcino', than I would run up, the first of all the other dogs, straight to the place that they had pointed the wolf out to me. I would charge across valleys, scour the hills, plunge into the thick forests, leap over the ravines, cross the roads, and return to the flock in the morning, without having caught sight of either the wolf or any trace of him; panting, exhausted, cut and bruised, with my feet pricked by thorns, only to find in the flock a dead sheep or a lamb slaughtered and half eaten by the wolf. I would despair at seeing how little purpose my care and diligence served. The owner of the flock would arrive, the shepherds would go out to meet him with the fleece of the dead animal, he would blame the shepherds for being negligent and order them to punish the dogs for being lazy, and they would beat us heartily with sticks.

And so, one day, having seen myself punished unjustly, and seeing that my care, nimbleness and bravery were of no use in catching the wolf, I resolved to change my tactics and not charge off in search of him, as was my custom, far from the flock, but to remain close to the flock, for since the wolf always came there, it would be the likeliest place to catch him. Every week the alarm was raised for us, and on one very dark night I caught sight of the wolves, more than the flock could be guarded against. I crouched down behind a bush, my fellow dogs rushed past and onward, and from there I kept watch, and saw two shepherds seizing one of the best lambs of the fold and kill it, in a way that made it truly look like the wolf had been its executioner. I was astounded, and I was equally amazed to see that the shepherds were the wolves and that those who were supposed to be guarding the flock were the same as those who were attacking it. They immediately informed the owner about the attack of the wolf, and gave him the skin and some of the flesh, keeping the biggest and best bits for themselves to eat. The master admonished them once again, and once again the dogs were punished. There were no wolves, the flock was decreasing in size, I so wanted to tell all, but I could not speak. All this filled me with wonder and grief. 'God help me,' I said to myself. 'Who can put a stop to this wickedness? Who has the strength to reveal that the defenders attack, that the sentries sleep, that those you trust rob you and that those who guard you kill you?'

SCIPIO: Very well said, Berganza, for there is no greater or craftier thief than the one on the inside, and as such those who trust are more likely to be killed than those who are cautious. The trouble, though, is that people can never get on well in this world if they have no trust and confidence in others. But let's not pursue this, for I don't want us to be seen as a pair of preachers. Pray continue.

BERGANZA: I shall indeed continue, and shall tell you that I then resolved to abandon that particular employment, despite the fact that it appeared so good, and to choose another which I might perform well in and in which, even if I was poorly rewarded, I would not be punished. I thereby returned to Seville, and entered into the service of a wealthy merchant.

SCIPIO: And how did you enter into his service? For, as far as things stand, it is very hard nowadays to find a decent man for your master. The masters of the earth are very different from the heavenly Master. Earthly masters, before receiving anyone into their service, pry into his lineage, examine his skills, inspect his appearance, and even want to know what clothes the fellow owns. However, to enter into the service of God, the poorest is the richest, the most lowly is the most high-born; and it is enough just to desire to serve Him with a pure heart for one's name to be placed in the eternal ledger of wages, which show themselves to be so generous that it exceeds even our utmost expectation.

BERGANZA: Well, that really is preaching, Scipio, my friend.

SCIPIO: Yes, I think so too, and therefore I shall be silent.

BERGANZA: Concerning what you asked me about the method I employed to enter into the service of my master, I shall firstly say that you already know that humility is the basis and foundation of all the virtues, and that without it there is no other virtue. Humility removes obstacles, overcomes difficulties, and is a means that always leads us to glorious ends. Humility makes friends of enemies, softens the anger of the irate and reduces the arrogance of the proud. In brief, with humility, vice can have no success, for in its mildness and gentleness the arrows of sin are dulled and blunted. I made full use of this virtue, therefore, when I wanted to enter into the service of any house, having first looked and made absolutely certain that the house was large enough to take in and accommodate a big dog. Then I would station myself at the door, and whenever by my reckoning a stranger went in, I would bark at him, and whenever the master of the house came I would lower my head and, wagging my tail, I would go up to him and lick his shoes. If I was sent away with a thrashing, I endured it, and with the same meekness I would once again butter up the one who had just thrashed me, for no one would be able to beat me a second time, having witnessed my perseverance and my noble behaviour. In this way, after two persistent efforts I would remain in the house. I would serve well and they would grow fond of me; nobody would dismiss me, unless it should be that I dismissed myself, or, better said, that I ran away. And who knows, but perhaps I had indeed found a master in whose house I would have still been today, if ill-fortune had not lain in wait for me.

SCIPIO: Using the same method that you have just mentioned, I too entered the service of the masters I have had. It's as if we could read each other's thoughts.

BERGANZA: If I am not deceived, we have indeed coincided in these matters, and, as I promised, I shall tell you about them later in their proper order. But for now, listen to what happened to me after I left the flock in the protection of those scoundrels. As I said, I returned to Seville, which is the refuge for the poor and a shelter for outcasts; which, in its great size gives ample room for both the poor and the rich alike. I stationed myself at the door of the grand house of a merchant, went through my usual performance and was soon received inside. They put me to work tied up behind the door by day and let loose by night. For my part I carried out my duties carefully and diligently; I barked at strangers and growled at those whom I didn't know very well. I never slept at night, doing my rounds of the courtyards, going up onto the terraces, becoming the universal sentry of my own and the neighbouring houses. My master was so pleased with my good service that he ordered that I should be treated well and that I should be given a ration of bread and the bones that were taken or thrown away from his table along with the leftovers from the kitchen. I showed myself extremely grateful for all this, jumping up and down at the sight of my master, especially when he returned from being away for a time. In these moments I expressed so much joy, and jumped up and down with such abandon that my master ordered that I should be untied, and that I should go loose by day and by night. Upon seeing myself untied, I ran up to him and ran around him several times, but without daring to lay my paws on him, recalling that fable of Aesop in which the ass was such an ass that he wanted to caress his master in the same way that the master's little dog caressed him, for which he received a sound thrashing. It seems to me that this fable serves to show us that what is graceful and becoming in one man is not in another. Let the jester tell his saucy jokes, let the clown juggle and do somersaults, let the rogue harp on, let the base man imitate the song of the birds and the various gestures and actions of animals and men if he so desires, but let not the man of rank and worth do these things, for none of these skills gives either merit or an honourable name.

SCIPIO: Enough, Berganza, I understand you. Please get on with it.

BERGANZA: Oh, if only those people I'm referring to understood me as well as you do; for perhaps due to my good nature it gives me great pain to see a gentleman act the clown, pride himself on being able to juggle balls, and claim that he surpasses everyone in dancing the chaconne. I know a gentleman who used to boast about how, at the behest of a sacristan, he had cut out thirty-two paper flowers to stick on a monument on black cloth, and how he was so impressed with these cuttings that he took his friends to see them, as if he were taking them to see the flags and spoils of his enemies placed over the graves of his parents and grandparents.

This merchant, then, had two sons, one of twelve and the other nearly fourteen, who were studying grammar in a college run by the Jesuits. They carried themselves proudly, always accompanied by their tutor and by pages who carried their books and the satchels known as the *vademecum*. Seeing them go about with such grandeur, in litters if it was sunny, in carriages if it was rainy, made me consider and reflect upon the great naivety with which their father would go to the Exchange to carry out his business, because he had no other servant than a Negro, and because often he would surpass himself by going on a shabby old mule.

SCIPIO: You should know, Berganza, that it is the custom and condition of the merchants of Seville, and even of the citizens, to demonstrate their authority and wealth not on their own selves, but on their sons, because the merchants are greater through the shadow they cast than through their own persons. And as only once in a blue moon do they concern themselves with anything other their mercantile affairs, they live a modest existence; and as ambition and wealth long to be shown off, these merchants dazzle through their sons. As a result they treat them and bestow honour upon them as if they were the sons of some prince. There are even some who procure titles for their sons, and place upon their breasts some badge which clearly distinguishes the important people from the plebs.

Berganza: It is ambition indeed, but an exaggerated one, to aim to better one's position without harming anyone else.

Scipio: Rarely, if ever, does ambition succeed if not through harming a third party.

Berganza: We have already said that we must not gossip and slander.

Scipio: Quite right, but I'm not gossiping about anyone.

Berganza: I've just this minute realised that it's true what I have often heard people say. A malicious slanderer has just ruined ten families and scandalised twenty good people, and if anyone reproaches him for what he has said, he replies that he has said nothing, but that if he *had* said anything, it was not intentional, and that if he had known that someone would be offended, then he wouldn't have said it at all. In all honesty, Scipio, anyone who wishes to maintain two hours of conversation and not enter even briefly into the world of gossip and slander needs to be very wise, and to tread very carefully; for I can see in myself that, being an animal such as I am, for every four things that I utter, words fly around my tongue like flies around wine, and all of them malicious and slanderous. For this reason I say again what I've said before: that acting and speaking badly are things we inherit from our first parents, and that we ingest them with our mother's milk, which is seen clearly enough in the fact that no sooner has the babe pulled his arm from out of his blanket than he raises his hand as if to take revenge upon anyone who, in his opinion, has offended him; and almost the first word he utters is to call his nurse or his mother a whore.

Scipio: Very true, and I must confess my error and ask that you forgive me for it, as I have forgiven so many of yours. Let bygones be bygones, as young lads say, and let us not have any backbiting from here on. Now carry on your tale, which you left hanging at the description of the haughty way the sons of your master the merchant went to the Jesuit College.

Berganza: I commend myself to Him above in everything, and although it's difficult for me to avoid gossiping, I intend to make use of a remedy that I heard was used by a person much given to swearing. He, repentant of his bad habit, after every regretted oath and curse, would pinch himself on the arm, or kiss the ground, as a penance for his sin. And so, every time I go against the appeal you have made to me, and against my intention not to gossip or slander, I shall bite the tip of my tongue so that it hurts, so that I am reminded of my sin and am urged not to do it again.

SCIPIO: This is such a remedy that, if you make use of it, I expect you'll bite so often that you will bite your tongue clean off, and then you will find it impossible to gossip.

BERGANZA: At least for my part I shall do my best, and may Heaven make up for my failures. And so I'll continue. One day the sons of my master left a folder on the patio, where I happened to be at the time, and as I had been taught by my former master the knifeman to carry his basket, so likewise I picked up the *vademecum* and ran after them, with the intention of not letting it out of my mouth until I arrived at the college. It all went exactly according to plan. My young masters, seeing me turn up with the *vademecum* held lightly by the straps in my mouth, sent a page to take it from me. However, I didn't allow him to do so, and did not let go of it until I entered the college, which made all the students laugh. I went up to the elder of my masters and, with great nobility, in my opinion, put it in his hands. Then I went and squatted down at the classroom door, intently watching the teacher reading at the lectern.

I don't know what it is about virtue, having little or no virtue myself, but I was deeply moved to see the love, the attention, the care and the effort with which those blessed fathers and teachers taught those young lads, straightening the crooked branches of their youth, so that those branches would not twist and turn to badness in the path of virtue, which they also taught them alongside the study of letters. I was impressed with how gently they scolded the boys, how mercifully they punished them, how they inspired them through example, encouraged them with rewards, helped them with wisdom and patience, and, finally, how they portrayed for them the horror and ugliness of vice and painted for them the beauty of virtue, so that, loving one and hating the other, they might achieve that purpose for which they were born and raised.

SCIPIO: You speak the truth, Berganza, for I have heard it said of these good people that as citizens of the world there are none in all of it as wise, and that as guides and leaders on the path to heaven there are none even comparable to them. They are mirrors which reflect honesty, the Catholic doctrine, divine prudence and, finally, profound humility, upon which the whole edifice of human happiness is based.

BERGANZA: It is all just as you say. And, to continue with my story, I'll recount how my masters desired that I always carry their *vademecum* for them, which I did very willingly, and as a result lived the life of a king, or perhaps even better than a king because it was a relaxed life. This was because the students took to playing with me, and I became so tame with them that they could place their hands in my mouth and the smallest of them could climb onto my back. They would throw their caps or hats and I would fetch them and return them to their hands nimbly and with a great show of joy. They took to feeding me whatever they had, and they liked to see how whenever they gave me walnuts or hazelnuts I would crack them open like a monkey, leaving the shells and eating the soft bit on the inside. There was even one who, in testing my skills, brought for me in a handkerchief a fair amount of salad, which I ate as if I were a human. All this was in wintertime, when in Seville you find buttered muffins, with which I was so well fed that surely more than one copy of Nebrija's book on grammar[7] was pawned or sold for my breakfast. In a word, I lived the life of a student without hunger and without the itch, which is all that you need to value so as to say that life is good; for if hunger and the itch were not such a part of the student life, there would be no more pleasing and entertaining life. For in the student's life virtue and pleasure go hand in hand, and one's youth is spent learning and enjoying oneself.

However, I was snatched out of this state of bliss and tranquillity by a lady who, I believe, is called in those parts a 'reason of state', whose demands you can only comply with by not complying with every other point of reason. The fact is that those college masters took it into their heads that the students were spending the half-hour period between classes not in revising their class notes, but in playing with me, and so they ordered my masters not to take me with them to school again. They obeyed, and took me home back to my old job as guard dog at the door. The old master, forgetting the favour that he had shown me in allowing me to run around untied by day and by night, put the chain back around my neck, and laid me on a mat that they had placed for me behind the door. Oh, my dear friend Scipio, if you could only know how hard it is to undergo the change from a happy state to a miserable one! Look, when misery and misfortune are lasting and continuous, they either kill you, or they become through their permanence a habit that you grow accustomed to enduring, which can help you to put up with even the hardest of them. Yet, when from a state of misfortune and calamity, one suddenly and unexpectedly enters a state of prosperity, joy and happiness, only to be plunged back into the former state of misfortune soon after, with its labour and hardship, well, it is a pain so intense that if it doesn't end your life, it's only so as to torment you more by making you live it.

So, as I was saying, I returned to my dog's rations and to the bones that the black girl of the house would throw for me, and even these were largely devoured by the savage cats which, being untied and nimble, easily snatched from me whatever did not fall within the limits of my chain. Scipio, my brother, may Heaven grant you all you desire, if, without your becoming upset, you allow me to philosophise a little now, because if I failed to say these things that have arisen in my memory now and which happened at that time in the past, I fear that my story would be neither complete nor of any use to anyone.

SCIPIO: Be careful, Berganza, that this urge to philosophise that you say has come over you is not the temptation of the devil; for slander has no better veil to cover up and disguise its dissolute evil than for the slanderer to be convinced that everything he says is a philosophical declaration, that to speak ill of someone is the same as reproof, and that to reveal the defects of others is a good and zealous deed. And if you examine and inspect attentively the life of any one of these slanderers, you will not find one that is not full of vice and insolence. And now that you know this, philosophise as much as you wish.

BERGANZA: Oh, you can be certain, Scipio, that I shall indeed philosophise more, for that is my intention. The fact is that as I was idle throughout the days, and as idleness is the mother of contemplation, I started going over in my mind those few Latin phrases that I remembered of the many that I heard when I used to accompany my young masters to college, with which, it appeared to me, I had grown in understanding and wisdom. I resolved, as if I already knew how to talk, to make the most of these phrases whenever the occasion arose, but not in the same way that ignorant people tend to use them. There are certain speakers of Spanish who, in conversation, let fly from time to time with some snippet of Latin, pretending to those who do not understand it that they are great Latin scholars, when in reality they scarcely know how to decline a noun or conjugate a verb.

SCIPIO: I see that as less harmful than those who really do know Latin, for there are some amongst them so foolish that, when talking to the shoemaker or the tailor, they throw in Latin phrases like water.

BERGANZA: From which we can infer that it is as sinful to use Latin in front of those who do not understand it as it is to use Latin without understanding it yourself.

SCIPIO: And there's another thing you should be wary of, and that is that there are people who, despite knowing Latin, are still plain ignorant.

BERGANZA: Well, who would doubt that? The reason is clear if you ask me; for when in Roman times everyone spoke Latin as their mother tongue, there must still have been some dullards amongst them who, despite speaking Latin, were still fools.

SCIPIO: To know how to hold one's peace in Spanish and talk in Latin one must be very shrewd, Berganza, my brother.

BERGANZA: Very true, for one can just as easily say something foolish in Latin as in Spanish, and I've seen educated fools, tedious grammarians and others who weave into their Spanish Latin phrases and words which can easily annoy everyone, not once but often.

Scipio: Well, let's leave this now, and please begin with your philosophies.

Berganza: But I've already said them – all those things that I've just been talking about.

Scipio: Which things?

Berganza: All that about the Latin and the Spanish, which I began and you finished.

Scipio: Ah, so you call gossiping 'philosophising'? That's wonderful! Dear Berganza, if you wished, you could even canonise this cursed plague of slander and gossip, and give it whichever name you desire; and gossip itself will call us all cynics, which means gossiping dogs.[8] But please be silent and carry on with your story.

Berganza: How can I carry on with the story if I'm silent?

Scipio: What I mean is that you should tell it all in one go, without making it appear like an octopus with all the tails you add to it.

Berganza: Speak properly: you don't say that an octopus has tails.

Scipio: That's the mistake made by the man who said that it was neither wrong nor rude to call things by their proper names, as if it were better, since one must name things, to refer to them by circumlocutions and roundabout phrases that lessen the repulsion caused by hearing their correct names. Honest words bear witness to the honesty of the one who utters or writes them.

Berganza: I'll readily believe that; and I'll carry on by saying that my fortune, not content merely to have snatched me from my studies and the happy and ordered life that went with them, and to have left me tied up behind the door, and to have bartered the generosity of the students for the meanness of the servant girl, ordered that I should be harried out of such peace and quiet as I had. Look, Scipio, take it for a fact, just as I do, that misfortune seeks out and finds the unfortunate one, even if he were to hide out in the world's darkest corner. I say that because the black girl of the house was in love with a black fellow, also a servant of the house, who slept in the porch between the front and the inner doors, and I lived behind this inner door. These two could only get together at night, and for this they had taken or forged the keys. And so most nights the girl would come down and, buying my silence with a bit of meat or cheese, would open the door to her fellow and have a grand old time with him. This was all helped by my silence and by the cost of the many things she had stolen. On some days these gifts of the servant girl rattled my conscience, as it was clear to me that without them I would be all skin and bone and would be taken for a greyhound and not a mastiff. But, in fact, led by my good nature, I resolved to repay what I owed my master, since I received his wages and ate his bread, just as you would expect not just an honourable dog with a reputation for gratitude to do, but all those who serve.

SCIPIO: Now this, Berganza, I would admit does pass for philosophy, since you employ reasoning of truth and understanding. Please carry on, and don't attach more threads, or indeed tails, to your story.

BERGANZA: First, though, I beg you to explain to me what the word philosophy means, if indeed you know, for although I talk of it, I'm not sure what it is. I only know that it is a good thing.

SCIPIO: I'll be brief in telling you. This noun is made up of two Greek nouns, being *philos* and *sophia*. *Philos* means 'love', and *sophia* means 'wisdom'. Therefore, *philosophy* means 'the love of wisdom', and *philosopher*, 'lover of wisdom'.

BERGANZA: You are very wise, Scipio. Who on earth taught you about Greek nouns?

SCIPIO: Berganza, you are in all honesty very simple if you are impressed by this. All schoolboys know this, and there are also those who pretend to know Greek but who, as with Latin, have no knowledge of it whatsoever.

BERGANZA: That's precisely what I would say, and I would like those people to be put in a press and the press turned until the juice of what they know is squeezed out of them, so that they don't go around deceiving everyone with the sham of their broken Greek and their false Latin, like the Portuguese do with the blacks in Guinea.

SCIPIO: Now, Berganza, you should bite your tongue, and I'll bite mine, for everything that we're saying is nothing but slander.

BERGANZA: True, although I'm not obliged to do what I heard a certain Corondas – a Tyrian – did.[9] He passed a law stating that

39

no one may enter the town hall bearing arms, under penalty of death. He himself forgot this law, and some days later entered the assembly wearing his sword. They pointed this out to him and reminded him of the penalty that he had decreed. Immediately he drew his sword and plunged it into his breast, thus becoming the first to place and break the law and the first to pay the penalty. What I said was not decreeing a law, but promising that I would bite my tongue whenever I gossip. Now, however, things are not as strict and severe as they were in ancient times. Nowadays a law is passed on one day and broken the next; and maybe it's better that way. Nowadays someone promises to mend their ways, and the next moment he has fallen headlong into far deeper sins. It's one thing to praise discipline but another thing to act along with it, and in fact between the word and the deed there's a wide chasm. Let the devil go bite himself, as I for one don't want to bite myself, or perform noble acts amongst these mats, where no one can see me who could praise my honour and determination.

SCIPIO: According to all that you say, Berganza, if you were human, you would be a hypocrite, and all your deeds would be a sham, a falsehood and a pretence, covered by the cloak of virtue, so that people may praise you, just as all hypocrites do.

BERGANZA: I don't know what I would do then. But one thing I do know now, and that is that I don't want to bite myself, leaving so many things unsaid that I don't know how or when I'll be able to finish them, all the more so as I fear that as soon as the sun rises we shall remain in darkness, having lost the power of speech.

SCIPIO: Heaven will be more kind to us. Carry on with your story and do not keep wandering off with these unnecessary digressions. In this way, however large the story is, you should get through it soon.

BERGANZA: Well, then – having seen the insolence, thievery and dishonesty of those black servants, I resolved, as a good servant should, to put an end to it, by the best means at my disposal. And sure enough I was well able to carry this out. The servant girl came down, as you've heard already, to sport with her fellow, secure in the knowledge that the bits of meat, bread or cheese that she chucked for me would keep me quiet. Bribes and gifts avail much, Scipio.

Scipio: Indeed they do, very much. Don't digress. Carry on.

Berganza: I remember that when I was studying I heard the tutor say a Latin proverb, which they call an adage. It went: *Habet bovem in lingua.*

Scipio: Good grief, what a time to drop in some of your Latin. Have you already forgotten what just a minute ago we were saying against those who slip Latinisms into their conversation in Spanish?

Berganza: Well, this piece of Latin fits very well here. You must understand that the Athenians used, amongst other things, coins stamped with the figure of an ox, and when a judge failed to do or say whatever was reasonable and just, because he had been bribed, they would say, 'This judge has an ox on his tongue.'

Scipio: I don't see the connection.

Berganza: Is it not clear? If the gifts of the black girl kept me quiet for many days, I didn't want or dare to bark at her when she came down for her liaison with her black lover. What I mean is that gifts and bribes can achieve a lot.

Scipio: And I have replied that indeed they can, and if it didn't cause a long digression now, I would prove with a thousand examples how much gifts can be worth; and perhaps I will, if Heaven grants me the time, the place and the power of speech to tell my own life story.

Berganza: May God grant you whatever you desire, and listen. Finally my good intention broke through the wicked briberies of the black girl, and, as she came down one very dark night to her usual pastime, I leapt at her without barking, so as not to awaken all those in the house, and in an instant I ripped to shreds her night-shirt and tore out a piece of flesh from her thigh, a stunt sufficient to put her to bed for more than a week, pretending to her master and mistress some sickness or other. She recovered and returned on another night. Once again I leapt at my little captive and, without biting her, I scratched her whole body as if she were wool to be combed. These battles were waged in silence and I always emerged from them the victor and the girl the victim, in rough

41

shape and increasingly angry. Well, her anger soon paid off upon my coat and my health, as my rations and bones were taken away from me. With no bones to gnaw, my own bones soon stood out along my back; but though they could take away my food, they could not take away my bark. The black girl, however, hoping to finish me off once and for all, brought me a sponge fried in lard. I recognised this evil trick and knew that I would sooner eat rat poison, for if you eat the sponge your stomach swells up and nothing, save death, will ever remove it. And so, realising that it would be impossible to protect myself from the traps and snares of such enraged enemies, I resolved to get out of their sight as quickly as possible.

One day I was not chained up and, without saying farewell to anyone of the house, I headed out into the street. Barely a hundred yards from the house by complete chance I ran into the bailiff that I mentioned at the beginning of my tale, who was a good friend of my former master Nicolás el Romo.[10] He immediately recognised me and called out my name. I also recognised him, and when he called me I went up to him with my usual performance of affection. He took me by the neck and said to two of his constables: 'This is a very famous guard dog who belonged to a great friend of mine. Let's take him home.' The men were delighted and said that if I was a guard dog I would be of great service to them all. They made to grab me in order to take me, but my master said that there was no need, as I would go willingly because I knew him. Ah, but I forgot to tell you that the steel-studded collar that I took with me when I fled from the flock of sheep was taken from me by a gypsy at an inn, and so I was collarless in Seville. But this bailiff put on me a collar studded with Moorish brass. Consider, Scipio, how the wheel of fortune turns: yesterday I was a student, today, you see me as lackey to a bailiff.

SCIPIO: This is the way of the world, and I think you've no need to exaggerate the twists and turns of fate, as if there were such a difference between being the servant of a slaughterhouse man or of a bailiff. I cannot bear and have no patience for hearing men complain about their fortune, whose greatest hope and ambition was to reach the level of squire. How they curse their accursed fortune! How they revile her with reproaches! And all this is merely so that anyone listening may think that they have fallen from the heights of good and prosperous fortune into the depths of despair and despondency that they see them in now.

BERGANZA: You are right, and I'll continue by saying that this bailiff was good friends with a notary, and the two of them would go around together. They had as their girlfriends two ladies of somewhat dubious morals. Well, the truth is they had pretty faces but much of the forwardness and craftiness that you see in whores. For their own type of fishing, the two men used these women as the net and the hook in the following manner: the ladies would dress in such a way that left nothing to the imagination about who they were, and from a mile off they showed themselves as women of easy virtue. They were always strolling around in search of foreigners, and whenever the great merchant fleet sailed into Cádiz or Seville, the scent of booty reached them, leaving not one sailor safe from their attacks. When one of these greasy men fell into the clutches of these fair ladies, they would let the bailiff and the notary know where they were going and the name of the house, and then, when they were together, these two would arrive and pounce on the foreigners and arrest them for consorting with prostitutes. Yet they never carted them off to the prison, for the foreigners always redeemed the offence with money.

It so happened, then, that Colindres – for that was the name of my master's lady – hooked a real greasy and grimy foreign sailor, who agreed to have dinner and spend the night with her in her lodging house. She slipped the news to her friend and, later, no sooner had they both undressed than the bailiff, the notary, two constables and myself all burst in on them. The lovers were startled and confused as the bailiff exaggerated the offence and ordered them to get dressed at once to be taken off to prison. The foreigner became greatly distressed, and the notary, moved through compassion and in response to the man's pleas, lowered the sentence to just one hundred *reales*. The foreigner asked for his chamois breeches that he had placed on a chair at the foot of the bed, in which he had the money to pay for his freedom. These breeches could not be found, of course, for when I had entered the room, a smell of ham reached my nostrils, which set me off like nothing else. I followed this scent to one of the pockets of the breeches, and inside I found a good piece of the best ham. In order to remove this piece and enjoy it without making any noise I took the breeches out into the street, and there I set upon the ham with great gusto. When I returned to the room I found that the foreign sailor was bellowing in some horrendous and weird but nevertheless comprehensible language that they must return his breeches to him, for he had fifty of the best golden escudos in them. The notary deduced that either Colindres or the constables had stolen them, and the bailiff thought the same. He summoned them aside, and they all swore on the devil that they hadn't done it. Seeing everything that was going on, I went back out into the street to where I had left the breeches in order to fetch them, for the money was of no use to me. But I couldn't find them, as some lucky passing fellow had taken them away. As the bailiff saw that the sailor had no money to pay the bribe, he became desperate, and threatened to get from the landlady of the house what he couldn't get from him. He called her and she came in half-dressed, and as she heard the shouts and complaints of the foreigner, saw Colindres naked and weeping, the bailiff in a blind fury, the notary angry and the constables pilfering whatever they could find in the room, she looked far from happy. The bailiff ordered her to go and get dressed and to accompany him to the prison for allowing men and women of loose morals in her house. Well, that was it! This really did set off a shouting match, and the confusion was greater than before, for the landlady said:

'Señor Bailiff and Señor Notary, do not try and play around with me and never attempt to pull the wool over my eyes, for I can see through all your tricks. Say nothing and leave this place. If you do not, I swear to God I'll raise merry hell and let the lid off this whole little affair. I know Señora Colindres very well, and I know full well that for some months you, Señor Bailiff, have been her "protector". Don't make me have to spell this out any clearer. Give this gentleman back his money, and we'll all be happy. For I am an honourable woman, and I have a husband with a patent of nobility bearing the official seal *a perpenan rei de memoria*, with its lead seals, praise be to God, and I perform my duties decently and cleanly without harming anyone. The price list of this house I have nailed to the wall where everyone may see it. So don't come moddling with me, as I know full well how to look after myself. And don't think that I'd be fool enough to allow my guests to bring women in with them. The guests have their own keys to their rooms. I'm no ferrous cat and I don't have the eyes to see through seven walls.'[11]

My masters were stunned at hearing how the landlady harangued them, and hearing that she knew all the details of their lives. However, seeing that she was the only one that they were going to get any money out of, they persisted in trying to cart her off to prison. She complained to high heaven about the unfairness and the injustice that they showed her, seeing that her husband, who was such a distinguished gentlemen, was absent. The foreigner, meanwhile, was bellowing for his fifty escudos. The constables insisted that they had never – God forbid such a thing – seen the breeches. The notary, whispering privately, was urging the bailiff to search through the clothes of Colindres, as he had the suspicion that she must have the fifty escudos, since she was well acquainted with rummaging through the pockets and hiding places of those who fell into her clutches. She insisted that the foreigner must be drunk and that he must have been lying about the money. In short, all was confusion, shouting and swearing, with no sign whatsoever of abating – and nor would anything have calmed down if at that moment the deputy of the magistrate, who had come to visit that lodging house, hadn't walked into the room, drawn by the shouts coming from within. He demanded to know the cause of all the shouting, and the landlady proceeded to tell him in the minutest detail, explaining all about the nymph Colindres, who was by now dressed. She revealed all about the public liaison between Colindres and the bailiff, she made known all about their tricks and their means of robbing, she exonerated herself, claiming that no woman of dubious morals had ever entered her house with her consent, she declared herself a saint and her husband a blessed man, and then she ordered a servant girl to run and fetch her husband's patent of nobility from a chest, so that the Señor Officer could inspect it, telling him that from this patent it would be clear to everyone that a woman with such a noble and honourable husband could never be accused of bad deeds, and that if she had the job of keeping a guesthouse it was because she had no other choice, for God knew how much it pained her, and that if she had but enough income and enough daily bread to rise above this profession then she would. The deputy, annoyed by the woman's endless prattle and pretensions of nobility, said to her:

'My dear landlady, I will willingly believe that your husband has proof of his noble lineage, if you will admit that he is a noble innkeeper.'

'And a very honourable one he is too,' replied the landlady, 'and what noble family is there in the world, however good, that does not have some secret or intrigue?'

'What I'm telling you, dear lady, is that you must get dressed and accompany me to the prison.'

This news shook her to the core; she scratched her face and screamed blue murder. But the deputy, despite all this, proved himself to be extremely severe, and carted them all off to the prison – that is: the foreigner, Colindres and the landlady. I later found out that the foreigner lost his fifty escudos and ten more besides, which they charged him for costs; the landlady paid as much again, and Colindres was released through the open door without charge. And on the very same day that they had taken her in, using the same little trick she hooked herself another sailor, who certainly made up for the other foreigner. So you see, Scipio, how much heartache and suffering were caused by my gluttony.

SCIPIO: Better to say by your master's knavery.

BERGANZA: Yes, but listen, for that was by no means their limit, although I don't like to speak ill of bailiffs and lawyers.

SCIPIO: Well said – yet speaking ill of one is not speaking ill of them all, for there are a great many lawyers who are honest, trustworthy and just, and who are keen to provide good results without harming a third party. Indeed, not all lawyers spin out the lawsuits, nor are they all hired by both parties in the case, nor do all lawyers take more than their dues, nor do they all go around making enquiries and prying into other people's lives so as to find something with which to accuse them, nor are they all buddies with the judge in a 'you scratch my back, I'll scratch yours' arrangement. Nor, indeed, do all the bailiffs make deals with vagabonds and crooks, nor do they all have mistresses like your master did for their little tricks and traps. There are many, very many of them who are gentlemen by birth and by nature, many of them are not rash, insolent, ill-bred, nor light-fingered, like those who go around the inns measuring the swords of foreigners, and if they find them a fraction longer than the legal limit then they ruin the owners. Indeed, not all of them catch people only to let them go, nor act like judges and barristers when they feel like it.

BERGANZA: Oh, but my master had his sights far higher than that, and his route was a different one. He thought of himself as something of a tough guy who could make dangerous arrests, yet he sustained this valour without any physical danger to himself, only to his purse. One particular day at the Puerta de Jerez he attacked six notorious villains, without me being able to help at all as I had a muzzle around my mouth which he would put on me during the day and take off at night. I was astounded by his bravery, his courage and his boldness, seeing how he leapt in and out of the six swords of the ruffians as if they were wicker straws. It was an astonishing thing to see the nimbleness with which he attacked, his sword thrusts, his parries, his judgement, and his eye alert to attacks from behind. In the end, in my opinion and in that of all the others who watched how he drove his enemies from the Puerta de Jerez to the marble pillars of the College of Mase Rodrigo, which is more than a hundred yards, he stood out to be a new Rodomonte.[12] He locked them up there, and returned to gather the trophies of the battle: three scabbards, which he then took to show the magistrate, who, if my memory serves me correctly, was at that time the Licentiate Sarmiento de Valladares, famous for the destruction of La Sauceda.

Wherever he walked through the streets, people would point him out as if to say, 'There goes the brave man who dared to fight single-handed against the hardest men of Andalusia.' The remainder of the day he spent walking around the city so as to let himself be seen, and that night we found ourselves in Triana, in a street near the gunpowder mill. Having done a quick recce (as they say in the slang of those parts) to check that nobody was watching him, he ducked inside a house with me following him. We came onto a patio and there were all the thugs of the fight, without swords or capes and with their shirts unbuttoned. One of them, who must have been the host, held a great jar of wine in one hand, and a large goblet in the other which he filled deeply with fine, lively wine, and toasted the assembled company. Scarcely had they seen my master than everyone rushed towards him with open arms and drank his health. He warmly accepted this, and returned it to everyone, and would no doubt have continued to do so many times over if there had been something in it for him, for he was a generous-hearted fellow who never wished to upset anyone for trivial things.

Oh, to tell you now about what went on there – the supper they ate, the fights they talked of, the robberies they referred to, the women who through their appearance and behaviour were of quality, and those whom they dismissed, the praises that they heaped upon each other, the absent toughs they named, the perfection of their fencing skills, the way some of them even got up in the middle of supper and, using their hands as swords, demonstrated these moves and feints, the rich and exotic vocabulary they used, and, finally, the impressive figure of the host himself, whom everyone appeared to respect as their lord and father – well, this would be putting myself in the depths of a labyrinth from which I wouldn't be able to escape even if I tried.

At length I discovered with certainty that the owner of the house, who was called Monipodio, was a protector of thieves and a comrade of ruffians, and that the great fight of my master had first been arranged through them, with all the details of fleeing and leaving the scabbards, which my master paid for there and then in cash, along with, later, the amount that Monipodio said that the dinner had cost, which lasted till daybreak and which they all enjoyed.[13] And by way of dessert they let on to my master about some tough rogue, recently arrived at the city and pretty dangerous, who must have been far braver than all of them as it was out of envy that they grassed on him. My master arrested him the following night, naked and in bed, and if he had been dressed it was clear to me from his build that he wouldn't have been taken with such assurance and ease. With this arrest, which followed on the heels of the fight, the fame of my cowardly master grew. And indeed he was a coward, more so than a hare, and for the price of free meals and drinks he fed his reputation for bravery, and everything he earned in his job and his secret dealings ran away down the drain of his pretended valour.

But be patient, and now listen to a tale of what happened to him, which I will not add to or subtract from even a comma. In Antequera two thieves stole a very fine horse, which they then brought to Seville and, in order to sell it, they used a ploy that, in my opinion, was most ingenious. They both went to stay at different inns, then one of them went to the magistrate and asked for a petition stating that Pedro de Losada owed him four hundred *reales* that he had loaned him, as testified by a receipt that he presented signed in his name. The magistrate ordered the said Losada to acknowledge the receipt and, if he did so, that he should either guarantee to pay back the sum, or be thrown in jail. It fell upon my master and his friend the notary to oversee this affair, and they took the thief to the inn where the other was staying, and he immediately acknowledged his signature, confessed the debt and offered the horse as guarantee of payment. My master took one look at the horse and resolved to own it, marking it for himself in the event of it being sold. The thief let the time allowed by law for the repayment to elapse, and the horse was put up for sale, with five hundred *reales* knocked down by a third party whom my master had arranged to buy it for him. The horse was in fact worth half as much again as what they paid for it, but as the seller's interests were in a quick sale, at the first bid he agreed to the sale. One of

49

the thieves collected a debt that was not owed to him, the other a receipt that was not warranted, and my master got his horse, which turned out to be worse for him than the horse of Seyano was for its owners.[14]

The thieves then decamped, and a couple of days later, when my master had sorted out the harness and other necessary gear of the horse, he rode out in the Plaza de San Francisco, looking more puffed up and pompous than a country bumpkin dressed for a feast day. He was congratulated heartily on his excellent purchase, and was assured that the horse was certainly worth one hundred and fifty escudos, as sure as an egg was worth a *maravedí*. He, meanwhile, strutting and parading the horse, played out his own tragedy in the theatre that was this aforementioned square. For, at the height of his turnabouts and prances, two fine-looking and well-dressed men arrived, one of whom cried out to the other:

'Well, strike me down, but that's Piedrahierro, my horse, which was stolen from me a few days ago in Antequera.'

All the four servants who accompanied him confirmed that this was true – that this was indeed Piedrahierro, the horse that had been stolen from him. My master was thunderstruck, the owner raised a great complaint and produced some proofs to justify his claim, which were so convincing that the judgement was passed in his favour, and my master was dispossessed of his horse. He at once realised the ruse and the cunningness of the thieves, who with the medium and intervention of justice had sold what they had stolen, and almost everyone else was delighted that the greed of my master had been his undoing.

And his misfortune did not end there, for that night the magistrate himself was doing the rounds, having been warned that there were thieves at large in the district of San Julián. As they passed a crossroads they saw a man running past, upon which the magistrate, seizing me by the collar and spurring me into a frenzy, shouted:

'Get the thief, Gavilán! Go on, boy! Get the thief!'

I, who by this stage was rather fed up of all the wickedness of my master, and in order to comply to the letter with the order of the magistrate, hurled myself at my own master and brought him to the ground before he knew what was going on; and if they hadn't pulled me off, I surely would have avenged his wrongdoings four times over. Well, they did pull me off, much to the regret of both the magistrate and me. The constables wanted to punish me, even to club me to death; and they would have done so if the magistrate hadn't commanded them:

'Nobody touch him, for the dog did exactly as I ordered.'

This vicious remark was understood by everyone, and I, without a by your leave from anyone, fled into the countryside through a hole in the city wall, and by dawn I had reached Mairena, a place about four leagues from Seville. By good fortune I fell in with a company of soldiers there who, as I heard, were off to board a ship at Cartagena. Amongst them were four thugs, friends of my master, and the drummer had been one of his lackeys; and a vulgar clown he was too, just like all drummers. They all recognised me and all asked me about my master as if I could reply. But the one who showed me most affection was this drummer, and so I resolved to stick to him, if he were willing, and to follow them even if this took me to Italy or to Flanders. I do believe, and so should you, that although the proverb goes, 'A fool at home is a fool abroad', visiting foreign lands and meeting different people can make a fellow wise.

SCIPIO: Too true, and indeed I remember having heard a very clever master of mine saying that the famous Greek named Odysseus was known for being wise simply because he had visited many lands and spoken to many people of diverse nations. Therefore I praise your resolve to travel to wherever these men might take you.

BERGANZA: Well, then, the fact is that the drummer, in order to have further clownish tricks to show off, began to teach me to dance to the drum and to perform other monkey tricks that no other dog than I would have been capable of mastering, as you'll hear as I continue. As they were nearing the end of their commission in that district, these soldiers were in no great hurry. There was no commissioning officer to keep us in check; the captain was a mere lad, but a gentleman and a good Christian; the ensign had only a few months before left the capital and the servants' hall in his master's house; the sergeant was astute and experienced, and skilled at driving the company from where it was raised to its point of embarkation. The company was made up of roguish deserters whose outrageous behaviour in the places we passed through brought curses down on one who had done nothing to deserve it. Surely it is the misfortune of the good prince to be blamed for the faults of his subjects, for it is never his fault that they fight each other. Indeed even if he wants to and attempts to, he will never remedy these evils; for nearly all things in war bring with them bitterness, hardship and suffering.

Anyway, in less than a fortnight, with my intelligence and the perseverance of my chosen master, I had learnt how to jump for the King of France and not to jump for the bad landlady. He taught me to leap and turn like a Neapolitan horse, and to plod round in circles like a mule in a mill, as well as other tricks, which, if I hadn't controlled myself against showing off prematurely, folk would have wondered whether it was some demon in the guise of a dog that was performing them. He gave me the name of 'the wise dog', and no sooner would we arrive at our lodgings than, beating his drum, my master would go around the whole place announcing that the marvellous and fabulous tricks, skills and feats of the wise dog were to be performed at such and such a house or such and such a hospital, and that anyone who wished to come and see them should do so at the cost of eight, or four *maravedís*, depending on whether the village was large or small. With these lofty public announcements, not a soul in the village would fail to show up for the performance, and not a soul would leave who was not impressed and delighted to have seen me perform. My master was overjoyed at the fortune he was making, and with it he kept six companions in a style fit for a king. Greed and envy awoke in the ruffians the desire to steal me, and they were always looking out for the opportune moment to do so, for earning one's living by doing very little is an occupation that has many supporters. For that reason there are so many puppeteers in Spain, so many who show picture tableaux, so many who sell pins and rhyming couplets – whose entire stock, if sold, would not raise enough to support them for a single day. And yet with this some of them never leave the bodegas and taverns all year, which leads me to believe that the money for their drinking must come from some source other than their occupations. All these people are idle, useless and worthless, soaking up wine like sponges and devouring bread like wolves.

SCIPIO: That'll do, Berganza, let's not regress to earlier. Please go on, as the night is soon to end and I wouldn't like the rising sun to plunge us into the darkness of silence.

BERGANZA: Fine, now listen. Seeing as it is easier to add to the invention than to invent from scratch, my master having seen how well I could imitate the Neapolitan steed, made me some coverings of embossed designed leather and a little saddle, which he fastened to my back. Sitting astride this, he placed an amusing figure of a man with a little lance like those used to tilt at the ring, and he taught me to charge straight at a ring hanging between two poles. On the day that I was to perform this, he announced publicly that the wise dog would today charge at the ring, and would perform other stunts never seen before, which, of course, I would have to make up on the spot so as not to make a liar out of my master.

Our daily progress, then, brought us to the town of Montilla, home of the famous and noble Christian, the Marqués de Priego, lord of the houses of Aguila and Montilla. My master was lodged, as was his request, in a hospital, where he set about making his usual announcements. As fame had travelled far in advance of us, bearing news of the skills and feats of the wise dog, in less than half an hour the patio was filled with people. My master was delighted to see that he was in for such a rich harvest, and that day he exceeded himself in his clownish performance. The show kicked off with me leaping through a hoop made from a sieve, which was more likely from a barrel. He goaded me on with the usual questions; and when he lowered a wicker cane held in his hand, that was the signal for me to jump, and when he raised it, for me to stay put. The first command of the day (the most memorable of my life) was:

'Come, then, Gavilán my boy. Jump for that dirty old man you know who dyes his whiskers. If you won't do that, jump for the pomp and show of Doña Pimpinela de Plafagonia, who in reality was the bosom friend of the Galician servant girl who served in Valdeastillas. So you don't like this command, eh, Gavilán my boy? Well, then, jump for Pasillas, the student who signs himself as licentiate when he has no degree at all. Oh, you lazy fellow! Why won't you jump? Ah, but I can see through your subtle tricks, yes indeed – jump for the wine of Esquivas, as worthy a tipple as that of Ciudad Real, San Martín and Ribadavia.'

He lowered the cane and I jumped, fully aware of his malice and wicked trickery. He then turned to the crowd and cried out in a loud voice:

'Do not think, my lords and ladies, that this dog only knows silly and frivolous tricks. Twenty-four tricks I have taught him, and a sparrowhawk would get up and fly for but the poorest of them. He can dance the *zarabanda* and the chaconne better than their original inventor. He can down a flagon of wine without spilling a drop; he can sing the *sol-fa-mi-re* as well as any sacristan. All these things, and many more that I still haven't mentioned, your lordships will see in the days that the company remains here. But for now, let our wise dog do one more jump, and then we'll get to the good stuff.'

At this he left his audience of 'lords and ladies' hanging on his words, all enflamed with the desire not to miss any of these tricks that I could perform. My master turned to me and said:

'Do it again, Gavilán my boy, with skill and with grace let's see you do those jumps that you've done before; but this time do them in devotion to the famous sorceress who is said to have lived in this place.'

Scarcely had he uttered these words than the hospital keeper, an old woman who looked more than seventy years old, cried out:

'Scoundrel, charlatan, cheat, bastard – there's no sorceress here! If it's Camacha you're referring to, she's already paid for her sins, and God knows where she is now. If it's me you're referring to, you reptile, I'm not nor have I ever been a sorceress. If I have the reputation for having been one, it is thanks to false witnesses, unwritten laws, and unjust and badly informed judges. Everyone here knows the life I lead, which is a penance not for the spells I never cast, but for my many other sins, which as a sinner I have committed. So, you sly loudmouth, get out of this hospital; and if you don't, by God, I'll drive you out quicker than you'd care to believe.'

With this she began to shout and scream and hurl such abuse at my master that he was left all shaken up and troubled. In the end, the performance was not allowed to proceed in any way. My master was not too put out by this disturbance, as he had already got all the money, and he postponed the remainder of the show for another hospital on another day. The people went away cursing the old woman, calling her not only a witch, but also a sorceress and a bearded old hag. Despite all this, we remained in the hospital that night, and when the old woman found me alone in the yard, she said:

'Is it really you, Montiel my boy? Can it by any chance really be you?'

I raised my head and gazed at her steadily. When she saw this, with tears in her eyes she came up to me and threw her arms around my neck and would have kissed me on the mouth if I'd let her, but that seemed revolting to me so I didn't let her.

SCIPIO: You did very well, for it is not a gift but a torment to kiss or be kissed by an old woman.

BERGANZA: What I'm about to tell you now I should have told you right at the beginning of my tale, for that way we wouldn't have had such reason for alarm at finding ourselves blessed with the gift of speech. For the old woman said to me:

'Montiel my boy, come along with me, and you'll see where my room is, and try to come tonight so that we can be alone there. I shall leave the door open for you, for I have many things to tell you concerning your life which will be to your advantage to hear.'

I lowered my head as a sign of obedience, by which she assured herself that I was indeed the dog Montiel that she had been looking for, according to what she told me later. I was bewildered and confused, eager for night to come in order to see where these mysterious or portentous words of the old lady were leading to;

and as I had heard her called a sorceress, I expected amazing things from seeing and speaking to her. Well, at length the moment arrived for seeing her in her room, which was dark, narrow and low-ceilinged, and lit only by the feeble light of a clay lamp. The old woman trimmed it and sat down on a small chest, beckoned me over and, without uttering a word, embraced me again; meanwhile I made certain that she didn't try to kiss me. The first thing she said to me was:

'Long have I hoped in heaven that I would see you again before these eyes of mine close for the last time, oh, son of mine. And now that I have seen you – come, Death, and carry me away from this weary old life. You must know, my boy, that the most famous sorceress in all the world lived in this town, she who went by the name of Camacha de Montilla. She was so unique in her profession that all the Ericthos, Circes and the Medeas,[15] who, I am told, fill the pages of history, could not match her. She could freeze the clouds whenever she wished and black out the face of the sun with them; and then when she so desired, she could make even the most turbulent weather clement. In a mere instant she could summon men from far-off lands; she could miraculously restore to maidens that which through their imprudence they had lost; she made dishonest widows appear honest; she could unmarry brides and arrange the marriages for those whom she chose. Around December she would have fresh roses in her garden, and in January she would reap wheat. Growing watercress in a trough was the least of what she could do, as was commanding the images of people, both living and dead, to appear in a mirror or in the fingernail of an infant. She had the fame of being able to convert men into animals, and of having been served by a sacristan for six years who, really and truly, had taken the form of an ass, which I've never fully understood. All those things that they say about those old sorcerers who turned men into beasts are said by those who know that it is nothing more than that these wise old women, with their beauty and their charms, attracted men with such force, subjecting them to such servility, demanding that they attend their every need to such a degree, that these men appeared to be animals.

'But in you, my son, experience shows me the contrary: for I know that you are a rational person, and I see you in the form of a dog, unless it is done by that magic that they call *tropelía,* which makes one thing appear to be another. Whatever the case, what grieves me is that neither I nor your mother, who were both disciples of the good Camacha, ever managed to know as much as she did; and not through lack of natural talent, or ability, or enthusiasm, of which we had too much rather than too little, but because of her excess of wickedness in never wanting to teach us the important things, wanting to keep them for herself.

'Your mother, my lad, was called Montiela, second only to Camacha in fame. I myself am called Cañizares, and if I didn't know as much as those two, I was no less eager to learn than them. The truth is that not even Camacha herself could match the determination your mother had to create and enter a circle, and then to close herself up in it with a legion of demons. I myself was always rather timid and scared: in conjuring up just half a legion I was content. Yet, with all due respect to those two, when it came to preparing the ointments with which we witches anoint ourselves, neither of them could match me, nor, indeed, could any of those who practise that craft today. And so, my lad, as I have seen and as I see now, that my life, which flies on the gossamer wings of time, is soon to end, I have wanted to abandon all the vices of sorcery in which for so many years I was engulfed, and all that I have left is the desire to be a witch, which is an extremely difficult vice to give up. Your mother did the same: she abandoned many vices and performed many good deeds in this life. But in the end she died a witch; not of any illness, but with the pain of knowing that Camacha, her teacher, was envious of her because she was getting to know as much as her, or because of some other quarrel of jealousy, of which I could never understand, when your mother was pregnant and on the point of giving birth. Camacha was the midwife, and as such she received in her hands that which your mother gave birth to; and what she held up for your mother to see were two puppies. Your mother, upon seeing them, cried out:

' "Oh, there's evil and trickery at work here."

'"Montiela, my sister, I am your friend, I will hide this offspring and you will concentrate on getting well. Rest assured that this misfortune of yours will remain entombed in silence. So do not grieve, for you know full well that I know that you have been only with your friend the labourer Rodríguez these past few days, and with no other. Therefore this canine offspring must be the issue of something else. There is indeed something mysterious about it."

'I (who had been witness to the whole bizarre business) and your mother were astounded. Camacha took the little dogs away with her, and I stayed to look after your mother, for she could not fathom what had happened. At length Camacha's end drew nigh, and as she was breathing her last she called for your mother and told her how she herself had converted the babes into dogs due to a certain quarrel that she had had with her, but that she shouldn't worry, as they would return to their proper nature when least expected; but that this could not take place until they themselves had seen with their very eyes the following:

> *They will return to their true form*
> *When they see how quickly and surely*
> *The haughty are brought down,*
> *And the humble are exalted*
> *By the hand that has the power to do it.*

'Camacha said this to your mother as she was dying, as I have already told you. Your mother wrote it down and engraved it in her memory, and I memorised it myself in case the time should come that I should have to say it to one of you; and in order to recognise you I call all the dogs of your colour that I see by the name of your mother, not because I think that the dogs will know the name, but to see if they reply when they are called by a name so different from those of other dogs. And this afternoon, as I saw you performing so many things, and as they call you 'the wise dog', and as you also raised your head to look at me when I called you in the yard, I have come to believe that you must be the son of Montiela. And it now gives me great pleasure to explain all about what happened to

58

you, and about how you can recover your original form, which I wish were as easy as they say it was for Apuleius in *The Golden Ass*, consisting merely in eating a rose.[16] In your case, however, it depends not on your own efforts but upon other people's actions. What you must do, my boy, is to commend yourself to God with all your heart, and wait for these divinations – I don't like to call them prophecies – to be fulfilled quickly and prosperously. For since it was the good Camacha who pronounced them, they will come about without a shadow of a doubt, and you and your brother, if he is alive, will see each other in the form you desire.

'What grieves me is that I am so near my own end that I shall not be able to witness it. Many times I have been tempted to ask my goat-demon how this affair of yours will turn out, but I have not dared to, because instead of giving a direct answer to questions, he always gives twisted and confusing answers which could mean anything. Accordingly, I should never ask my lord and master anything, as to every one truth he mixes a thousand lies; and from what I have gathered from his replies, he knows nothing concrete about the future, and as such can only guess. Yet despite all this, he has us witches so fooled that, although he constantly tricks and deceives us, we cannot leave him. We go to see him in a large field a long way from here, where a large group of us gathers – witches and wizards alike – where he gives us tasteless and insipid food to eat, and where other things happen which in truth and in God's name I dare not recount, for they are so dirty and disgusting that I would hate to offend your chaste ears. Some people are of the opinion that we only go to these gatherings in our imagination, and that in our fantasy the devil shows us the images of all those things that we later say have taken place. Others disagree, saying that we do go in body and soul. For my part I believe both opinions to be correct, because, seeing that all that takes place in our imagination is so intense and vivid that we cannot distinguish it from when we really and truly go, we do not know whether we go in one particular way or in the other. Certain experiments relating to this have been carried out by the gentlemen of the Inquisition upon some of us they have taken captive, and I think that they have found that what I say is true.

'I would like to give up these sinful ways, my son, and therefore I have done several things: I've managed to become matron of this hospital, I look after the poor, and the death of one of them provides quite a living for me because of either what they bequeath me or what they leave amongst their rags, which I take great care to pick clean; I pray a little, in public; I slander people a great deal, in secret; it is better for me to be a hypocrite than an outright and declared sinner. The good works which I do openly and publicly are gradually erasing from the memory of those who know me the evil deeds of my past. Basically, feigning saintliness damages nobody other than the one who feigns it. Look, Montiel my boy, this is the advice I'll give you: be as good as you can, but if you must be bad, do your best not to let it show. I am a witch and I do not deny it; your mother was both witch and sorceress, which I also cannot deny to you, but our good appearances gave us good credit in the opinion of everyone. Three days before she died we had both been at a large gathering in a valley in the Pyrenees, and, even so, when she died it was with such calm and peacefulness that, if it weren't for some grimaces that she made a quarter of an hour before surrendering her soul, one would have thought she was lying on a bed of flowers. She grieved for her two sons deep in her heart, and even in the throes of death she would not pardon Camacha, such was her determination and resolution in things. I myself closed her eyelids and accompanied her to her grave. There I left her, never to see her again, although I have not lost all hope that I may see her before I die, for it is said in the area that some people have witnessed her walking abroad in different forms around the cemeteries and roads. Perhaps I shall come across her some time, and then I shall ask her if she wants me to do anything to put her conscience at rest.'

Each of these things that the old woman told me in praise of the woman she called my mother was like a lance that pierced my heart, and I felt like attacking her and tearing her to pieces with my teeth, and if I refrained from doing so it was because I did not want her to die in such a bad state. Finally, she informed me that she was planning that night to anoint herself and attend one of the usual gatherings, where she would ask her master for any information about what was to happen to me. I wanted to ask her about the anointing oils she mentioned, and she appeared to read my mind, as she responded to my thoughts as if I had really asked the question, saying:

'These oils with which we witches anoint ourselves are made up of the juices of herbs which are extremely cold and which, contrary to what the masses say, are not made of the blood of the children we have throttled. Here you may also ask me what pleasure and profit the devil has in making us kill these tender creatures, since he knows that, being baptised and being innocent and free from sin, they will go straight to heaven, and that he suffers tremendous pain with every Christian soul that escapes him. Well, I can only reply by referring to the proverb that says: "There are some who would lose both eyes so that their enemy loses one"; in other words, because of the anguish that parents suffer when he kills their children, for it is the worst pain imaginable. And what the devil wants more than anything else is that we should commit the most cruel and perverse of sins at every step. It is because of our sins that God Himself allows all this; for without God's permission I know from experience that the devil cannot harm even an ant. This I saw to be true when once I implored him to destroy the vineyard of an enemy of mine, and he replied that he could not so much as touch a single leaf of it, because God would not allow him to do so.

'You will realise when you are a man that all the disasters and misfortunes that fall upon people, kingdoms, cities and towns – the sudden deaths, the shipwrecks, the downfalls – in short, all the misfortune that is seen as accident, all comes from the hand of the Almighty and with the consent of His will; whereas the evil and strife that are seen as having an author come from and are caused by ourselves alone. God is impeccable, from which we must realise that we are the authors of sin, forming it in our intention, in our words and our deeds; and God allows this, as I have already stated, because of our sins. You'll now ask yourself, my son – if indeed you are able to follow me at all – who made me a theologian; and perhaps you'll say to yourself: "Curse the old whore! Why doesn't

61

she stop being a witch, if she knows so much, and turn to God, for she knows that he is quicker to forgive sin than to allow it?" To this I would reply, as if you had already asked it, that the habit of a vice becomes second nature, and this vice of being a witch becomes part of our flesh and blood; and with all its ardour, which is strong, it brings such a coldness to the soul that it chills and dulls the soul even in its faith, from whence arises such a forgetfulness of itself that it recalls neither the punishment which God threatens, nor the glory which He invites it to share. Moreover, as it is a sin of the flesh and of pleasure, it necessarily deadens the senses, and charms and absorbs them, leaving them unable to be employed as they should. And so the soul is rendered useless, powerless and spiritless, unable to summon up the will to consider even one good thought; and so, allowing itself to be plunged into the depths of misery, it refuses to reach out and take the hand of God, which He offers through His pure mercy so that the soul may rise. I myself possess one of these souls that I describe to you. I see all this and I understand it, but as pleasure has seized my will, I am and always will be a bad person.

'However, let's leave this and return to the business of the anointing oils. As I said, they are so cold that they deprive us of all our senses when we anoint ourselves with them, leaving us lying naked on the floor; and then, as it is said, we go to experience in our imagination all those things that we believe are really happening. On other occasions just after applying the oils, it seems to us that we change form, and, converted into cockerels, owls or crows, we go to the place where our master awaits us, where we recover our original form and enjoy pleasures that I shall not describe for you, as they are such that my memory is appalled at the mere recollection of them and my tongue shrinks from telling them; and that's with me being a witch, covering my many faults with the cape of hypocrisy. And sure enough if there are some people who esteem and honour me as a good woman, there are many who insult me to my face with every imaginable name – names that have stuck to me ever since an enraged judge in the past dealt with your mother and me, placing his fury in the hands of the executioner, who, because he wasn't bribed, employed his full power and authority upon our bare backs.

'But this has passed as all things pass; memories fade, the dead do not come back to life, tongues get tired of gossip and new events make us forget past events. I am now matron of the hospital, my good behaviour is outwardly manifest; my oils give me many enjoyable moments; I am not so old at seventy-five that I cannot hope for another year. And seeing that I cannot fast due to my age, nor pray due to my weakness, nor go to religious celebrations due to my feeble legs, nor give alms due to my poverty, nor think good thoughts due to my love of gossip (and in order to do good it is necessary to be able to think it first); my thoughts, therefore, are bound to be always bad. Despite all this I know that God is good and merciful and that He knows what is to become of me – and that is enough for me. But let's leave this type of talk, which truly makes me sad. Come, my boy, and watch me anoint myself, for all pain can be borne with bread, let's enjoy it while we can, for while we laugh we do not weep. What I mean is that, although the pleasures the devil gives us are transparent and false, they are nonetheless pleasures, and an imaginary pleasure is far better than an actual one, although with true and authentic pleasure the opposite ought to be the case.'

She got up upon making this lengthy harangue, took the lamp and went into another narrower room. I followed her, afflicted by a thousand troublesome thoughts, and amazed at what I had heard and what I expected to see. Cañizares hung the lamp on the wall and rapidly undressed down to her shift. Then she took a glass bowl from a corner, put her hand in it, and, muttering something under her breath, anointed herself from her feet up to her uncovered head. Before finishing anointing herself she told me that whether her body remained, unconscious, in that room, or whether it disappeared, I should not be alarmed, but should remain waiting there until the morning, for then I should learn about the things I had to do in order to become a man. I lowered my head in agreement and she completed her anointment and laid herself out on the floor as if she were dead. I brought my nose up close to her face, and noticed that she was scarcely breathing at all.

There's one thing I must confess to you, my dear friend Scipio. I was truly frightened to find myself shut up in that tiny room with that figure in front of me, which I shall describe to you as best I can. She was more than seven feet long, all bones like a skeleton, covered in a black, hairy and leathery skin. Her stomach, which looked like a sheepskin, hung down over her private parts, reaching almost beyond her thighs. Her nipples resembled a pair of dried-up and wrinkled cow's udders; her lips were blackened, her teeth clamped tight, her nose was hooked and misshapen, her eyes bulging out of their sockets, her hair was ruffled, her cheeks sunken, her neck scrawny and her breast withered. In short, she was all skin and bone and looked like the devil himself. I began slowly to examine her and was suddenly gripped by a fear in seeing the terrible appearance of her body and in considering the worse occupation of her soul. I wanted to bite her to see if she would regain consciousness, but I couldn't find a single part of her whose vileness did not repulse me. However, I took hold of one of her heels and dragged her into the yard, but even with this she did not show any signs of recovering her senses. Out there, looking up at the sky and seeing myself surrounded by wide, open space, I lost my fear, or at least my fear lost enough of its hold on me to allow me to wait and see the outcomes of the comings and goings of that wicked woman, and what she would tell me of my affairs. On this matter I asked myself, 'Who made this wicked old woman so wise and yet so evil? Where did she learn about the evil that is the will of God and the evil that we bring on ourselves? How does she understand and talk so much about God, and yet do so much of the devil's work? How is it that she sins so much through wickedness without being able to excuse herself through ignorance?'

The night passed while I pondered over all this, and the new day found us both in the middle of the courtyard, she still having not regained consciousness and I still crouching next to her, alert, watching her frightful and hideous appearance. The people of the hospital turned up and, witnessing that scene, some of them said:

'So the blessed Cañizares is dead. See how disfigured and wasted away her penances have left her.'

Others, more perceptive, took her pulse and, finding that she still had one and was not dead, assumed that she was in a state of ecstasy or in a trance, due to her goodness. There were still others who said:

'This old whore is doubtless a witch and has doubtless anointed herself, for saints never experience such shameless trances; and up to now, amongst those of us who know her, she's had more fame as a witch than as a saint.'

There were some curious folk who went up to her and stuck pins in her flesh, from head to toe, yet not even this brought her to her senses, nor indeed did she awaken until seven in the morning. Finding herself riddled with pinpricks, bitten on her heels and bruised from being dragged out of her room, and as there were so many eyes staring at her, she believed, correctly, that I had been the author of her dishonour; and so, charging at me and grabbing me around the neck with both hands and trying to strangle me, she shouted:

'Oh, you scoundrel, you ungrateful, ignorant and malicious rogue. Is this how you repay the good deeds I did for your mother, and that I intended to do for you?'

I saw myself in grave danger of losing my life between the claws of that wild harpy, so I freed myself and seized her by the folds of her stomach, shook her and dragged her across the yard, while she screamed and shouted to be released from the teeth of that evil spirit.

These complaints of the wicked old woman made most of those present believe that I must be some kind of demon who continually persecutes good Christians, and some ran up to sprinkle me with holy water. Others were too afraid to pull me off her, and others shouted out that I should be exorcised. The old woman growled and snarled and I clamped my teeth firmer together. The confusion increased and my master, who had turned up having heard the noise, was in despair at hearing people call me a demon. Others, who knew nothing about exorcisms, ran up armed with three or four clubs, with which they began to beat me on the back. I soon tired of this painful game, so I let go of the old woman, and in a leap and a bound I was off down the road and out of the town, pursued by a gang of young boys shouting: 'Keep clear, the wise dog has gone mad!' Others, however, were saying: 'He's not mad. He's the devil in the form of a dog!'

Having received such a pounding, I fled the town, followed by many who, as much because of the tricks they had seen me perform as because of the words that the old witch had uttered when she awoke from her wretched sleep, undoubtedly believed that I was the devil. Indeed, so quickly did I flee from their sight that they believed that I had vanished like the devil. In six hours I had covered twelve leagues, and at length I arrived at a camp of gypsies in a field near Granada. There I was able to recover a little, as some of the gypsies recognised me as the wise dog, and with no little display of joy welcomed me and hid me in a cave so that I should not be found if anyone came looking for me; and with the intention too, as I later found out, of making some money through me as my master the drummer had done. I was with them for twenty days, during which time I got to know and noted their life and their customs, which, since they are worthy of note, I will relate to you now.

SCIPIO: Wait, Berganza. Before you proceed, we had better return to those things the witch said to you in order to ascertain whether this big lie that you give credit to could possibly be true. Look, Berganza, it would be the greatest folly to believe that Camacha could transform men into beasts and that her sacristan served her so many years, as people say, in the form of a donkey. All these things and other similar things are lies, deceits and fabrications of the devil; and if it seems to us now that we have some power of understanding and reason, seeing as we are talking when we are in fact dogs, or at least have the form of dogs, we have already established that this is a portentous and unprecedented case, and that although it appears to be really happening, we should hold our judgement until the outcome of the situation convinces us to believe in it. Do you want me to make that any clearer? Just think about how foolish and stupid were the things Camacha said that our restoration to human form depended on. Consider also those things that to you must appear prophecies but which are no more than proverbs and old wives' tales, like those tales of the headless horse and the magic wand with which people entertain themselves around the fireside during the long winter nights – for, if they were anything else, they would have already been fulfilled. Unless, of course, her words should be interpreted in what I have heard called an allegorical sense, which means that the words do not mean what they seem to say, but something that, although it may appear similar, is in fact completely different. In this way, if you say:

They will return to their true form
When they see how quickly and surely
The haughty are brought down,
And the humble are exalted
By the hand that has the power to do it,

and you interpret it in the sense I've mentioned, it seems to me that what it means is that we will recover our true form when we witness how those who yesterday were at the top of the wheel of fortune, today are fallen and trampled under the feet of misfortune, and held in low esteem by those who once esteemed them. And in the same way, when we see that others who not even two hours ago had no purpose in the world other than adding to the quantity of people that dwell in it, they are now so high and lofty in praise and respect that they have risen out of sight; and if at first they were invisible through being so small and insignificant, now we cannot keep up with them through being so great and exalted. And if our restoration to our true form, as you say, depended upon this, well, we've already seen it and continue to see it at every step. As a result, we are not to interpret the words of Camacha in an allegorical sense, but in the literal sense. Yet not even in this sense is our remedy to be found, for countless times we have witnessed what the words say, and we are still, as you can see, very much dogs. Therefore I declare that Camacha was a false joker, Cañizares a deceitful liar, and Montiela a stupid, malicious scoundrel, begging her pardon should she in fact be our mother, or rather yours, as I for one wouldn't want her for a mother. What I'm saying, therefore, is that the true meaning of it all is like a game of skittles, in which the pins are quickly knocked down and then promptly put back upright by the hand that is able to do so. Think, therefore, about how many times in the course of our lives we will have seen a game of skittles, and how many times because of this we have been changed back into men, if indeed we are men.

BERGANZA: Scipio, my dear brother, I own that you are right in what you say, and that you are more perceptive and wise than I had imagined. From what you say, I am inclined to think and believe that everything that has happened to us up to now, and what we are experiencing now is a dream, and that we are, indeed, dogs. But because of this let us not fail to enjoy this gift of speech and this excellence of human discourse for as long as we are able; and so don't lose interest in listening to my account of what happened to me with the gypsies who hid me away in the cave.

SCIPIO: With great pleasure I shall continue to listen to you, so that you will listen to me when, if Heaven grants it, I tell you the events of my life.

BERGANZA: The life that I led with the gypsies made me consider at that time their ample malice, treachery and trickery, and their thieving, which is carried out as much by the women as by the men, and practised from the moment they leave their cradles and start to walk. Have you seen how many of them there are scattered across Spain? Well, they all know each other and know what each is up to, and they move about and exchange and switch the stolen goods around hither and thither. They obey one they call the Count with greater loyalty than they would obey the King. They give him, and all who succeed him, the nickname of Maldonado; and not because they are of the noble lineage of this name, but because the page of a certain gentleman of this name fell in love with a gypsy girl who denied his love unless he became a gypsy and took her for his wife. The page accordingly did this, and this pleased the other gypsies so much that they made him their leader and promised to obey him; and as a sign of their allegiance they offer him a share of the things they steal, if these things are of any value. In order to have something to do in their idleness, they make things out of iron, such as instruments useful for their thieving; and therefore you will always see in the streets the menfolk selling things like pliers, drills, hammers, and the womenfolk selling trivets and fire shovels. Every gypsy woman is a midwife, and in that they have an advantage over our women as with no cost and with no assistance they can deliver their children, immediately washing the newborn in cold water. And so, from birth until death, they become hardened to suffering and can endure all the inclemency and rigours of the heavens, being, as you'll have seen, hardy and robust, and good jumpers, runners and dancers. They only ever marry amongst themselves, so that their bad customs are not revealed to outsiders. The women honour and respect their husbands, and there are very few of them who would ever offend their husbands with non-gypsies. When they beg for alms, they receive them more through their elaborate stories and coarse jokes than through piety and devotion; and using the excuse that no one ever trusts them, they never work but rather seek a life of idleness. Moreover, if I remember correctly, scarcely ever have I seen a gypsy woman at the foot of the altar receiving communion, and I have been in churches often. Their thoughts are wholly taken up with planning how to trick and deceive people, and where the next robbery will take place; and they all tell each other about their robberies and how they carried them out.

In this way, one day a gypsy in front of me was telling the others about a trick and a robbery that he had once carried out upon a labourer. The story went that the gypsy had a donkey with a very short tail, and to this hairless stump he attached a hairy tail with hair that looked like the donkey's own. He then took it off to the market and sold it to the labourer for ten ducats. Having sold the beast and received his money, he asked the labourer if he wanted to buy another donkey, the brother of this one and just as good – he would sell it to him at an even better price. Well, the worker asked him to go and fetch it, as he would certainly buy it, and said that while the gypsy was gone he would take this one that he'd bought to his lodgings. Off he went and the gypsy followed him and was somehow skilful enough to steal back the donkey that he'd just sold to the fellow, and promptly take off its false tail, leaving the donkey with the hairless stump. He then changed the saddle and the bridle and had the cheek to go looking for the labourer in order to sell it to him. He found him before he'd noticed the loss of his first donkey, and with no fuss the fellow bought the second donkey. The worker then went to his lodgings to get the money, where, finding no donkey, he realised that he himself was the donkey. So, although based only on a hunch, he suspected that the gypsy had stolen the beast and refused to pay him. The gypsy went in search of witnesses and returned with those who had received the tax payment of the first sale of the donkey, and they all swore that the gypsy had sold the labourer a donkey with a very long tail, and very different from the second beast that he was selling. All this of course was witnessed by the bailiff, who took the side of the gypsy to such a degree that the labourer was forced to buy the same donkey twice over. They told many other tales of robberies – all, or most of them, involving animals, for this is the field in which they are most knowledgeable and practised. In conclusion, they are a bad lot, and although many a wise judge has brought sentence upon them, this does not make them change their ways.

After twenty days they decided to take me to Murcia. I passed through Granada, where the captain whose drummer was my master was already stationed. As soon as the gypsies found out about this, they shut me up in a room of the inn where they were staying. I heard them talk about the reason for this and none of it appeared at all good to me, so I resolved to escape. I succeeded in this and, fleeing Granada, I came to an orchard that belonged to a Morisco[17] who took me into his service willingly. I now found myself in a far better state, as it appeared to me that he would want nothing more of me than to guard his orchard – a job which, in my opinion, required less labour than guarding livestock; and as the issue of salary was never called into question, it was easy for the Morisco to find a servant to command and for me a master to serve. I ended up remaining with him for more than a month, not because I particularly enjoyed the life I led, but because of the pleasure I received in learning about the life of my master and, through this, the lives of all the Moriscos who live in Spain. Oh, the things I could tell you, Scipio, my friend, about this Morisco rabble, if I weren't afraid that doing so would take me two weeks to finish! And if I were to go into each individual case, I wouldn't finish in two months. But, nevertheless, I will say something, so listen to what I saw in general, and what I noted in particular about these good people.

It would be a pure miracle to find just one out of the many of them who truly believe in the sacred Christian laws; all they are concerned about is making huge amounts of money, and piling up the money they have made, and to do this they work but never eat. As soon as a coin of any value comes into their possession, they sentence it to life imprisonment and perpetual darkness; and so, by the means of constantly earning and never spending, they acquire and amass the largest quantity of money that exists in Spain. They are, indeed, their own money-box, moth, magpie and weasel – they acquire everything, they hide everything and they swallow everything. Just think about how many of them there are, and that every day they earn and stash away something, either a lot or a little, and that a slow fever will kill you just as surely as the plague; and that as they increase in number so does the number of hoarders and hiders increase, and they grow and will continue to grow ad infinitum, as experience shows. Amongst them there is no chastity, and neither men nor women enter into religious service; they all marry, they all multiply, because sober life increases the chances of propagation of each generation. War does not consume them, nor does any job tire them too much; they steal from us calmly and silently, and with the fruits of our inheritance, which they sell back to us, they make themselves a fortune. They have no servants, for each is his own servant; they waste no money on their children's education, for the only knowledge they need is how to rob us. Of the twelve sons of Jacob who, I have heard, entered into Egypt, Moses brought out of captivity six hundred thousand men, not including women and children; from which you will imagine how these women will multiply since they are incomparably more in number.

SCIPIO: Remedies have been sought to resolve these evils that you have broadly identified and outlined, for I know full well that the evils you do not mention are greater and worse than the ones you do, but up to now no suitable remedy has been discovered. Wise guardians, however, look after our republic who, knowing that Spain breeds within its bosom as many vipers as Moriscos, will find, with God's help, a sure, prompt and effective solution for such an evil.[18] Carry on.

BERGANZA: Well, seeing that my master was so stingy in everything, just as all his breed are, he kept me alive with millet bread and watery gruel, his own daily fare. But Heaven helped me to bear this daily misery in a very peculiar way, which you will now hear. Every morning with the sunrise, a young man would be found sitting at the foot of the many pomegranate trees of that orchard. He looked like a student, wearing a baize gown, which was no longer black and plush, but discoloured and moth-eaten. He would spend his time writing in a notebook, and from time to time he would slap his forehead and bite his nails while staring up at the heavens. Other times he would take on such a pensive air that he moved neither hand nor foot, not even an eyelash, so lost was he in thought. One day I went up to him without him noticing me; I heard him mutter something to himself and, after quite a while, he shouted out in a loud voice:

'God be praised! That is the best octave verse I have written in all the days of my life!'

Hastily writing in the notebook, he expressed tremendous signs of happiness, by which I worked out that the poor wretch must be a poet. I sidled up to him with my customary acts of tenderness to demonstrate to him my tameness, and I lay at his feet; while he, reassured by this, continued in his musings, scratched his head again, lost himself in his trance, and began once again to write all that he had composed. While he was thus engaged, another young man, elegant and well dressed, came into the orchard, carrying some papers in his hand from which he was reading from time to time. He came up to the first fellow and said:

'Have you finished the first act?'

'I've just completed it,' replied the poet, 'and it is the most elegant that you could imagine.'

'In what way?' asked the second fellow.

'In this way,' replied the first. 'His Holiness the Pope appears, dressed in pontifical attire, with twelve cardinals all dressed in purple. The events of my play, you see, take place at the time of the annual re-robing known as the *mutatio caparum*, when cardinals dress not in red but in purple. Therefore it is entirely right and proper that my cardinals appear wearing purple; and this is a very important detail of my play upon which people would certainly pick up and make a thousand rude and facile comments. There is no possible way that I've made a mistake in this, as I have ploughed through the complete book of Roman ceremonial just to get this matter of dress correct.'

'And where,' replied the other, 'do you imagine that my stage manager is going to get hold of purple robes for twelve cardinals?'

'If he so much as leaves out just one of the robes,' replied the poet, 'I'd sooner grow wings than give him my play. For heaven's sake, is this grand and splendid spectacle to be wasted? Just imagine the scene in the theatre as the Supreme Pontiff appears with twelve solemn cardinals and other ministers who absolutely must be in attendance. Good grief, it would be one of the best and most glorious spectacles to have been seen on stage, better even than *Ramillete de Daraja*.[19]

At this point I worked out that while one was a poet, the other was an actor; and this actor then advised the poet that if he didn't want to make it impossible for the manager to stage the play, he ought to cut out that bit about the cardinals. The poet's response to this was to state that they ought to be grateful that he hadn't included the whole conclave that would have attended the memorable ceremony and which would have made such an impression on the audience watching this most excellent of plays. The thespian laughed at this and left the poet to his business while he departed to his own, which was studying the script of a new play. The poet, after writing a few more verses of his magnificent play, calmly and slowly took out of his satchel some chunks of bread and a handful of about twenty raisins. I say twenty for that's as many as appeared to my counting, but it may have been fewer as they were all stuck together with breadcrumbs. He blew the breadcrumbs off the raisins, and proceeded to eat them one by one, including the stalks, as I never saw him chuck any of them away, helping them down with bits of bread which, covered in purple fluff from the satchel, seemed to be mouldy. They were so hard that although he tried to soften them by chewing, he could not succeed in doing so at all, which, however, turned to my advantage, as he tossed them to me, saying:

'Here, boy! Take this and enjoy it!'

'Well, just look at the nectar or ambrosia this poet gives me,' I said to myself. 'They say that this is what the gods and Apollo feed on up there in the heavens!'

Basically, the life of the poet is for the greater part one of misery, but even more so was mine, as I was obliged to eat what the poet threw away. During the whole time that he was working on his play he never failed to turn up at the orchard, nor did he fail to chuck me the scraps of bread, for he shared them with me with great generosity; and then we would go down to the water pump, where, me flat on my belly and he with the aid of a jug, we would quench our thirst like kings. Finally, however, the poet did not return, and I became so overcome with hunger that I resolved to leave the Morisco and go into the city to seek my fortune, for nothing ventured nothing gained. As I entered the city, I saw my friend the poet coming out of the famous monastery of San Jerónimo. Upon seeing me, he came rushing towards me with open arms, while I went up to him with a great show of affection at having found him again. Then he immediately proceeded to take out pieces of bread, much softer than the bread he usually took to the orchard, and to place them in my mouth without putting them in his own first, an act of tenderness which doubly satisfied my hunger. These soft bits of bread and the fact that the poet had come out of the monastery I've just mentioned made me suspect that his muses were as shamefully hungry as the muses of other poor poets. He started off into the city and I followed him, resolved to serve him if he were willing to be my master, and imagining that with the leftovers from his castle my camp would be supplied, for there is no greater or more generous purse than that of charity, whose liberal hands are never poor. As such I do not agree with the proverb that goes, 'The hard-hearted man gives more than the hard-up man', as if the miser would give as much as the poor yet generous man, who will at least always give you his best wishes if he has nothing else to give.

Moving from one place to the next, we eventually came to the house of a manager of plays called Angulo el Malo, not the other Angulo, who is one of the most entertaining actors on stage either then or now. All the company gathered around to hear my master's play, for I now considered him master. Yet by halfway through the first act, one by one and two by two they all began to walk out, leaving just the manager and myself as the only audience. Although I am an ignorant ass in matters of poetry, the play was such that it seemed to me that Satan himself had written it for the total ruin and perdition of the poet, whose mouth had already dried up at seeing the solitude in which his audience had left him. Perhaps, indeed, his soul had foreseen and warned him of the dire disgrace that now threatened him, for just then all the actors returned, more than twelve of them, and without a word they seized my poet and, were it not for the authority of the producer, who pleaded and shouted, they would no doubt have given him a dreadful tossing. I was dumbfounded by what I'd seen: the manager enraged; the bunch of comedians delighted; and the poor poet thoroughly depressed. With great patience but with a bitter look on his face, the poet then took his play, tucked it into his breast and, half muttering, said, 'One should never cast pearls before the swine.' Having said that, he very calmly walked away.

I myself was so ashamed that I was unable to follow him; nor did I want to, and in this I made the right decision, because the manager stroked and patted me so much that I felt compelled to remain with him. In less than a month I had become an enormous hit with my comic routines and mimes in the intervals. They put a fancy muzzle on me and they taught me to attack on stage any chosen character, and in this way, seeing that these sketches invariably end with beatings and scuffles, in my master's company they usually spurred me on to such a degree that I would assail and bring down everyone, which made the ignorant mob roar with laughter and brought great profit to my master. Oh, Scipio! If I could only tell you the things I witnessed there, and in other companies that I joined. But as there is no way I'd be able to reduce it to a succinct and brief narrative, I'll have to leave it for another day; if indeed there is to be another day in which we can communicate with each other. Do you see how long my discourse has been? Do you not see the many and diverse experiences I've had? And do you not appreciate the number of roads I've walked down and the number of masters that I've served? Well, all that you've heard is nothing compared to what I could tell you about what I noted, confirmed and saw of these people, their lives, their customs, their occupations, their leisure, their ignorance, their wit, along with countless other things, some only to be told in private, others to be proclaimed in public, and all of them to be remembered by those people who need awakening from idolising fictitious characters and illusory beauties of artifice and transformation.

Scipio: I can see only too clearly, Berganza, the wide space that lies open for the unfolding of your discourse. Yet I am strongly of the belief that you'd do better to leave it as a separate story, to be related leisurely and without fear of interruption.

Berganza: Very well, but listen. I came with a company of actors to this city of Valladolid, where in one of the performances I was wounded so badly that I nearly lost my life. There was no way I could take revenge, as I was muzzled, and because I did not want to do so in cold blood, for premeditated revenge denotes cruelty and a wicked heart. I became tired of that occupation, not because of the work, but because I was forever seeing in it things that needed to be reformed or even punished; and as my lot was only to see and not to remedy anything, I resolved not to see them any more. And so I sought refuge and sanctity, as do all those who abandon their vices when they cannot practise them, although it's better to do so late than never. By this I mean that, seeing you one night carrying the torch with the good Christian Mahudes, I reckoned that yours was a happy, just and righteous occupation; and full of healthy envy I resolved to follow in your footsteps. With that praiseworthy intention I stood in front of Mahudes, who at once chose me for your companion and brought me to this hospital. The things that have happened to me here are by no means so insignificant that they don't deserve their own time and space to be related, especially the details of what I heard from four patients whom fortune and necessity brought together in this hospital in four beds adjacent to each other. Forgive me, but this story is brief and cannot be shortened in any form and, moreover, fits in here perfectly.

SCIPIO: Of course I'll forgive you, but do conclude soon, as I fear daybreak is not far off.

BERGANZA: Well, then, in the four beds that are towards the rear of this ward, there was an alchemist in one bed, a poet in another, a mathematician in another, and in the last bed one of those political theorists known as *arbitristas*.

SCIPIO: Yes, I remember having seen some of these good people.

BERGANZA: Well, during a siesta some time last summer, when all the windows were closed and I was lying under one of the beds, soaking up some cooler air, I heard the poet start to complain miserably about his fortune, and when the mathematician asked him what he was complaining about, he replied that it was because of his meagre luck.

'And do I not have good reason to complain?' he continued, 'for having religiously followed the dictates of Horace in his *Ars Poetica* that I should never release my work to the public until ten years after writing it, I have a work that took me twenty years to write, and which I finished twelve years ago. The work is profound in its subject matter, new and admirable in its inventiveness, ponderous in its verse, entertaining in its episodes, and measured in its pace and structure, for the beginning is tied both to the middle and to the end. In this way the poem is lofty, sonorous, heroic, pleasing and substantial; and yet, with all this, can I find a prince to whom I can dedicate it – a prince who is intelligent, liberal and magnanimous? Oh, it is a miserable and depraved age that we live in.'

'What's the book about then?' enquired the alchemist.

'It concerns,' replied the poet, 'the things that the Archbishop Turpin never managed to write about King Arthur of England, including a supplement called *The Account of the Search for the Holy Brail*. [20] It is all in heroic verse, part in octave and part in free verse, yet all in dactylic stress; that is, with this dactylic stress lying on the nouns and not on a single verb.'

'As for myself,' replied the alchemist, 'I scarcely know anything about poetry, and as such am unable fully to appreciate the misfortune of which you complain. Your misfortune, however, even were it far worse than you say, would never come close to mine; for, through lack of instruments or a prince to support me and provide me with the things that the science of alchemy requires, you do not see me now rolling in gold and richer than any Midas, Crassus or Croesus.'[21]

'Señor Alchemist,' asked the mathematician at this point, 'have you at any stage performed the experiment of extracting silver from other metals?'

'Up to now I have not done so,' replied the alchemist. 'But I do know for a fact that it can be extracted, and I myself am only two months away from finding the philosopher's stone, with which one may extract silver and gold even from stones.'

'You fellows have greatly exaggerated your misfortunes,' said the mathematician at this point. 'For at the end of the day one of you has a book to dedicate to someone, and the other is very close to finding the philosopher's stone. What, therefore, can I tell you about my misfortune, which is so unusual that it can find no support or favour? For a full twenty-two years I have been searching for the fixed point. One day I've found it, the next day it's gone; and when I think that I have found it, and that it can never escape me, suddenly and unexpectedly I'm amazed to find myself miles from it. It has been the same thing with my attempts to find the quadrature of the circle, in that I have been so close to achieving it that I don't know how or why I don't have it already in the bag. My suffering is equal to that of Tantalus who, though near to the fruit, is dying of hunger and, though near to the water, is dying of thirst. At moments I think I shall hit upon the moment of truth, and at other moments I feel so far from the truth that I have to climb back up the same mountain that I've just descended, with the weight of my work on my shoulders, like some latter-day Sisyphus.'

The *arbitrista* had until this point maintained his silence, but now he broke it, saying:

'Poverty has brought together in this hospital four of the greatest moaners the world has seen, who complain so much that you'd think the Great Turk himself were the cause of their problems. For my part I renounce jobs and occupations that neither entertain nor provide daily bread for those who practise them. Good sirs, I am an *arbitrista*, a political theorist, and at many different times I have put forward to His Majesty different theories and schemes, all for the benefit and not the harm of his realm. I have now drafted a petition in which I entreat him to let me know of a person to whom I may communicate a new theory of mine, a theory so important that it would benefit all the King's interests. However, seeing what has happened to other petitions of mine, I fear this one will be cast in the ditch with the others. But so that you gentlemen don't take me for a simpleton, and even though in doing so my theory will be made public, I wish to explain to you what it is.

'The Cortes[22] must rule that every one of His Majesty's subjects between the ages of fourteen and sixty must fast on just bread and water once a month on a day that they specify. All the money that would have been spent that day on other foods such as fruit, meat, fish, wine, eggs and vegetables should, under oath, be handed to His Majesty without holding back a single coin. By doing this, he will have no need for schemes to raise money and will be freed from his debts. For if one adds it up, as I have done, you see that there are well over three million people of this age living in Spain, not in-cluding the sick, the old or the young, who never spend more than at least one and a half *reales* on any given day. Indeed I'm asking for no more than one *real*, as you could only live on less by eating hay. Well, do you gentlemen not think that having three million *reales* harvested each month is a fair enterprise? What's more, this would be of great benefit and not harm to the people who fast, for in fasting they please God and serve their King, and each would be able to fast in a way that is good for his health. This is the essence of my theory, and the payments could be collected within the parishes, without the cost of administrators who cripple the state.'

Everyone laughed at both the scheme and the schemer, and he himself laughed at his far-fetched theories. I was greatly bewildered to hear these men and see that, in general, men of that cast of mind came to die in the hospitals.

SCIPIO: You're quite right, Berganza. Have you any more to say?

BERGANZA: Just two things, no more, and then I'll stop talking, for I think the dawn is approaching. One night my master went off to beg for alms at the house of the chief magistrate of this city, who is a gentleman and a good Christian. We found him alone, and because of this it seemed to me a highly opportune moment to tell him about certain words of advice that I had heard an old patient of the hospital say concerning how to resolve the notorious problem of the street girls who, rather than work, take up this wicked life, which is so wicked that in summer all the hospitals are full of the wretched men who have gone with them. It is an intolerable plague, which calls for an immediate and effective solution. As I said, I wanted to tell him all this, and so I raised my voice, thinking that I could speak. Yet instead of declaring wise words of reason, I barked so hastily and so loudly that the magistrate, annoyed, ordered his servants to come and beat me away. One of these lackeys answered his master's call (if only he'd been deaf), and seized a copper jug that was to hand and dealt me such a blow to the ribs that I still bear the marks of that beating today.

SCIPIO: And did you not complain, Berganza?

BERGANZA: How was I not going to complain, if even now I can feel the pain of a punishment that my worthy intentions never deserved?

SCIPIO: Look, Berganza, no one should meddle in affairs where he's not been called, nor concern himself with jobs that are not his. Besides, remember that the advice of the poor man, no matter how worthy, is never accepted; and that the poor and humble man should never presume to counsel the great and those who think they know it all. Wisdom in the poor man is hidden and obscured in the shadows and the mists of want and necessity, and if by chance this wisdom is revealed, it is judged as stupidity and treated with contempt.

BERGANZA: You're right, and henceforth I shall follow your advice and learn from my mistakes. Another night, likewise, I went into the house of an important lady, who had in her arms one of those little dogs that are known as lapdogs, so small she could hide it in her bosom. This tiny bitch, when it saw me, leapt out of the arms of its lady and charged at me, barking with such boldness that it didn't stop until it had bitten one of my legs. I turned to look at it with caution and some anger and said to myself:

'If I were to catch you in the street, you horrible little creature, I would either ignore you altogether or I would rip you to pieces with my teeth.'

I reflected at seeing her that even the cowards and the faint-hearted become daring and insolent when they can curry some favour through it, and are quick to insult those who are more worthy than them.

SCIPIO: We can see the honest truth of what you say in those meagre fools who in the shade of their masters dare to be insolent, and if some chance death or other mishap of fortune brings down the tree they lean against, well, their lack of valour is clearly visible, for, in fact, their pretence at lustre and worth is entirely dependent upon their masters and protectors. Virtue and wisdom are always one and the same thing, naked or dressed up, alone or accompanied. It is true that people may at times judge them to be of lower esteem, but never is the truth of their merit and value lessened. And with this, let us bring an end to our conversation, for light is shining through those cracks, revealing that we are already well into the new day; and tonight, if this wonderful gift of speech has not abandoned us, it will be my turn to tell you my life story.

BERGANZA: So be it, and make sure you come to the same spot.

The licentiate finished the colloquy and at the same time the ensign woke up. The licentiate then said:

'Even if this colloquy were made up and never actually took place, it is in my reckoning so well written that, my dear Señor Ensign, I entreat you to continue with the second.'

'What you say,' the ensign replied, 'will stir me to get down to writing it, without further disputes with you about whether the dogs actually spoke or not.'

To this the licentiate replied:

'Dear Ensign, let's not return to that argument. I can perceive the artifice of the colloquy and its inventiveness, and that is enough. Let's go to the Epsolón[23] and entertain our eyes, seeing as we have now entertained our minds.'

'Very well, let's be off,' said the ensign.

And with this, they departed.

NOTES

1. Here Cervantes creates a pun from the words *casamiento* (marriage) and *cansamiento* (tiredness).

2. The *Puerta de la Carne* (Meat Gate) was so called in reference to the abattoir.

3. San Bernardo was an area of Seville near the abattoir, where many of the slaughtermen lived.

4. The list of names appears as an ironical take on the lofty and classical style of contemporary pastoral work, with characters appearing from works of Lope de Vega (1562–1635), Luis Gálvez de Montalvo (1549–1610) and Jorge de Montemayor (1519–61). With splendid irony, Berganza includes 'Elicio', a character from Cervantes' own pastoral romance *La Galatea* (1585).

5. Mauleón was a historical poet renowned for being dim-witted.

6. 'God of gods' (Latin).

7. Antonio de Nebrija (1444?–1522) published his vastly influential *Arte de Gramática* in 1481. He also compiled a popular Latin dictionary.

8. Scipio here is making (and explaining) a pun on the word *cínico*, 'cynic'. The word comes from the Greek *kunikos* or *kynikós*, declined from the noun *kuōn, kunos,* or *kyon, kynós*, meaning dog, from which comes the Latin *canis*.

9. Berganza erroneously refers to the anecdote related by both Diodorus Siculus and Valerius Maximus. 'Corondas, a Tyrian' should read, 'Charondas from Thurii'.

10. Berganza overlooks or forgets that he never in fact mentioned the bailiff at the beginning of the tale.

11. The landlady mispronounces many of the things she utters. The phrase *a perpenan rei de memoria* should read *a perpetuam rei memoriam*. This was originally a papal seal which became commonplace on documents of lineage. She later says 'quince' (fifteen) for 'lince' (lynx). See also 'moddling' and 'ferrous'.

12. Rodomonte, the Saracen warrior in Boiardo's *Orlando innamorato*, was ironically famed not for his bravery, but for his arrogance.

13. The character Monipodio appears in the same guise in another of *Las Novelas ejemplares* of Cervantes, *Rinconete y Cortadillo*.

14. This refers to an obscure legend of a Roman named Sejanus whose horse brought misfortune on himself and on all who subsequently rode it.

15. These are all witches or sorceresses in classical mythology.

16. Apuleius (b. AD 123) was the author of many works, including *The Golden Ass*, in which the character Lucius is transformed into an ass, then changed back into a man by the goddess Isis, through the eating of a rose.

17. The Moriscos were moors baptised as Christians following the Reconquest. With the religious fervour of the age, the Moriscos remained a marginalised and persecuted society. Between 1609 and 1614, Felipe III, influenced by the Duke of Lerma, ordered the expulsion of the Moriscos. Several hundred thousand were expelled, and most of them moved to North Africa. The expulsion of the Moriscos contributed to the crippling of Spain's

economy. In literature and theatre the Morisco was often the figure of ridicule.

18. Irony is perhaps present in Scipio's vehement comment. By mentioning the Moriscos in the same sentence as vipers, Berganza may be implying that where a mass cull of snakes is a futile gesture, so was the move to expel such a body of people. Cervantes, moreover, treats the Moriscos sympathetically in *Don Quixote*.

19. *Ramillete de Daraja* was a famous play dealing with Morisco life, of unknown authorship and now lost. It is mentioned by numerous writers of Cervantes' time, most notably Quevedo.

20. His mistake here exposes his false erudition.

21. Midas was a Phrygian King cursed with the power of changing everything he touched into gold; Crasssus was a Praetor of Rome, powerful because of his wealth; Croesus, the last King of Lydia, possessed proverbial wealth.

22. Spanish parliament.

23. A plaza near the river in Valladolid, and a place for the evening *paseo*.

BIOGRAPHICAL NOTE

Miguel de Cervantes Saavedra was born near Madrid in 1547. His family was impoverished and forced to travel frequently in search of work. After studing for several years in Madrid, in 1570 Cervantes journeyed to Rome, where he spent a short time working for Cardinal Giulio Acquavita and studying Italian literature and philosophy. In the same year he joined a Spanish regiment at Naples and fought in the naval battle of Lepanto, where he was injured in the left hand and given the nickname, 'the cripple of Lepanto'.

Cervantes remained in the military until 1575, when his ship was captured by pirates and he and his brother Rodrigo were sold as slaves in Algiers. He lived as a slave for five years – an experience which inspired his first play *El Trato de Argel* [*The Traffic of Algiers*] (1582–7) – until the ransom for his release was finally raised by his family. He returned to Madrid, and embarked on a series of poorly paid and unsuccessful administrative jobs. In 1585 he married Catalina de Salazar y Palacios, though the marriage was childless and lasted less than five years.

The remaining years of Cervantes' life were spent as a tax collector and purchasing agent. The work was fraught with legal difficulties and he was imprisoned for financial irregularities on at least two occasions. It was during his second imprisonment, in La Mancha (1602), that he is said to have composed the first part of his greatest work, *Don Quixote*, a satire on contemporary chivalric romances.

Cervantes' literary output in the early part of the seventeenth century was prolific; he composed mainly prose works, which ensured his widespread contemporary fame and his enduring reputation. His financial and social situation remained permanently unsteady, however, and at one point his entire household was imprisoned on suspicion of the murder of a nobleman who died outside his front door. In 1615 Cervantes produced the second part of *Don Quixote*, in response to a spurious sequel published by another writer, and three days after completion of his final novel, *Los Trabajos de Persiles y Sigismunda* [*The Exploits of Persiles and Sigismunda*] (1617), he died.

William Rowlandson is a lecturer on Spanish language, translation, and Spanish and Latin American literature at the University of Exeter. He has published articles concerning the work of Borges, Neruda and Cabrera Infante, and plans to publish his doctoral research concerning the Cuban author José Lezama Lima.